x-24: unclassified

a collection of short stories

EDITED BY
Tash Aw *&* **Nii Ayikwei Parkes**

x magazine / lubin & kleyner

an x magazine paperback
co-published by lubin & kleyner, london

First Published in the United Kingdom 2007.

This anthology is typeset in Lacuna, a font created by Glashaus
Design, and Palatino from Linotype GmbH
Printed and bound in Great Britain by Cromwell Press, Trowbridge, Wilts

ISBN-10: 095415701X
ISBN-13: 978-0954157012

Supported by
 **The National Lottery**®
through Arts Council England

Acknowledgements

The editors express thanks to the Arts Council of England for its financial assistance. They are particularly grateful to Sarah Sanders and Charles Beckett at the London office for their guidance and support. For clearance to use copyrighted material they are indebted to:

Peter Hobbs for 'Waterproof' from his collection *I Could Ride All Day in My Cool Blue Train* (Faber, 2006)

Laila Lalami and Liz Maples for 'The Saint' from Laila Lalami's *Hope and Other Dangerous Pursuits* (Algonquin Books of Chapel Hill, 2005)

Mohammed Naseehu Ali for 'The Prophet of Zongo Street' from his collection *The Prophet of Zongo Street* (Amistad Press, 2005)

Daniel Alarcón for 'Republica and Grau,' previously published in the *New Yorker*.

Contents

Introduction

Anyone who moves to a big city such as London to try to establish themselves as a writer will very quickly become aware of the number of other young writers doing the same thing. The sheer breadth of the cultures these writers represent is at once exciting and terrifying: how on earth does one jostle one's way to the top of the heap? How and where does one even begin?

Most new writers hone their craft by writing short stories ('*surely* easier to get published than a novel'), but outlets for even the best short stories are limited. Newspaper and magazine space devoted to short fiction seems always to be dominated by well-established literary figures, not the mathematical unknown, x.

X-24 is a collection that attempts, in its small way, to celebrate and promote short fiction by emerging writers. It is an anthology that has its roots in X, an independent London-based magazine founded by Nii Parkes that seeks to provide writers a platform for their early work. With X-24 we wanted to showcase the astonishing range of writing cultures we have come across whilst working on X magazine, cultures that, regardless of distance, affect us all.

The majority of writers whose work appears in X-24 come from non-Anglo-American backgrounds, and at least half do not live in London. All the writers represented here are at the start of their careers; some have already established considerable reputations for themselves whilst others publish for the first time. Above all we have selected a group of writers from around the world who represent some of the most exciting new writing around.

Tash Aw & Nii Ayikwei Parkes

SEFI ATTA

Green

THIS IS GOING to be really boring. I forgot my book in the car. We are in the immigration office in New Orleans. The television is on CNN not Disney. A news woman is talking about the elections again. I don't vote. I'm only nine.

We sit in plastic purple chairs joined together, Mom and me. Dad stands in line for one of the booths. The booth curtains are purple too. They are open like a puppet show is about to begin, but real people sit behind the glass windows, stamping and checking. I hope my parents get their green cards. I really hope we can drive back to Mississippi in time for my soccer game.

Booth A is for information and questions. Booth B is for applications. Booth C is for replacement cards. D is for forms and E is for adjudications. I know these words because I read, especially when I'm bored. What I don't understand is why must they explain the rules in different languages here?

No Smoking is *No Fumar*

No Drinking is *Khong Duoc Uong*

No Eating is *No Comer* and *Khong Duoc An*

I ask Mom, "What language is that?"

"Spanish," she says. She is not wearing her glasses so she can't see far. She is holding the yellow envelope for their passports.

I should have guessed Spanish. I take lessons in our after-school program. Mr. Gonzalez won't let us leave until we get our words right. He is always telling us to shut our mouths or else. Then you should see him at mass on Thursdays, eating the body of Christ and drinking the blood of Christ.

There are people here who look like Mr. Gonzalez. Indian-looking people too, like my friend Areeba, who left our school because Catholic religion was confusing her. There are people who look Chinese to me, but whenever I say this, Mom says, *They're not all Chinese!* Sometimes she gets on my last nerve. I'm just a kid. There is one family who looks African like us, but Mom says they must be Haitian because a man next to them keeps speaking French to their son.

A pretty woman comes out of a wooden door. "Mr. Murphy?" she says. "Enrique Morales?" The third name she says sounds like Hung Who Win?

Mr. Murphy is the French-speaking man. "*A bientot*," he says, when he gets up. No one in the Haitian family answers him. Maybe they are too tired to be polite.

I tell Mom, "Bet that's where the green cards are hidden. Behind that wooden door."

"Like lost treasure," she says.

"Why green?" I ask.

"I don't know."

"Maybe because green is for go?"

"Maybe."

"Remember when you ran a red light, Mom?"

"When did I ever run a red light?"

She did. She ran one and said it was too late to stop. I was small and I yelled, "Oo, that's against the law."

"Can I please go and get my book from the car?" I ask. "Please?"

"No," she says. "Absolutely not. What if they go and call us?"

Green is for vegetables. I will never eat mine. Green is for Northeast soccer field, especially when it rains. Green is for envy. My best friend Celeste is trying to make a move on my man, just because their names both start with C. His name is Chance. I told Mom my true feelings when she forced me to share. She said if two women are fighting over a man they've already lost. "What if your best friend makes a move on your man?" I asked. "Kai," she said and bit her finger. "I blame that Britney Spears."

Dad hands over their passports to an old woman with orangey lipstick in the booth. When he comes back, he sits next to me.

"How long will it take?" I ask.

"You never know," he says.

"What if it takes all day?"

"We'll wait."

"Aw, man."

"Aw man, what?"

"Nothing."

Last year, when Grandpa died, Dad couldn't go for the funeral in Africa. Mom said this was because they were out of status waiting for their green cards. If Dad went to Africa, he wouldn't be able to come back to America. Dad cried. Mom said people didn't know the sacrifices we had to make. Then on the day of Grandpa's funeral, a white pigeon landed on our roof. She said that it was Grandpa coming to tell Dad his spirit was at peace, which made me scared, so I sneaked into their bed again, in the middle of the night, even though I really didn't believe that pigeon on the roof was my Grandpa.

"How I wish we can get back to Mississippi before six," I say.

"What's on at six?" Dad asks. "Some Disney rubbish?"

"Never mind," I say.

If I tell him, he'll think I'm selfish. I want to get back to Mississippi in time for soccer. Already he is watching the elections on CNN.

Green is for my parent's passports. Green-white-green is the color of the flag of their country in Africa, Nigeria.

* * *

THE PRETTY WOMAN comes out of the door again. What she says sounds like *Oloboga? Ologoboga?*

"That's you," I say, pulling Dad's jacket. "Come on. Come on."

"Ah-ah, what's wrong with you?" he asks.

"Calm down," Mom says.

Sometimes my parents act like I'm bothering them all the time. I walk behind them. I don't even want to be in the same footsteps with them. The pretty woman says, "Hey, Sweetie."

"Stop sulking," Mom says.

"Are we getting your thumbprint today, Sweetie?" the pretty woman asks me.

"No, she's the American in the family," Mom says and smiles.

On the other side of the door, I don't see any green cards, only a room with a table and a copier. The pretty woman does Dad's thumbprint, then Mom's, and then she writes our address in Mississippi to send their green cards. Mom won't stop thanking her.

"You have no idea. We waited so long. When will they come?"

The woman leads us to the door saying, "By regular post. Yes, you can travel as you like. Yes, yes, you're officially permanent residents." I don't think she cares.

"Can we go now?" I ask, after she shuts the door.

The Haitian family is still sitting out there. The lines for the booths are longer. An Indian boy spreads his arms like plane wings and makes engine sounds with his lips. *Brr! Brr!*

We walk to the elevators.

"Mardi Gras parade," Dad says.

"Is there one this afternoon?" Mom asks.

"Shall we?" he says. "To celebrate?"

"Do you want to stay for a Mardi Gras parade?" Mom asks me.

Dad is dancing. Limbo. The yellow envelope with their passports is under his armpit. It's so embarrassing.

"Em," I say. "No."

Last year we came for Mardi Gras in New Orleans. The weather was sunny. We watched the Oshun Parade on Canal Street. I was trying to catch the beads people were throwing from the floats. I preferred the golds. My neck was weighed down. Mom kept yelling in my ear, "Oshun is African. People here don't know. She is the Yoruba goddess of love." Her breath smelled of the beignets we ate for breakfast. Dad was saying, "Don't just reach out like that. That's why you keep missing them. See, there is a technique to catching the beads." "What technique?" Mom asked and Dad stepped in front to show us and a huge black bead smacked him in the face. Then we had to eat lunch. I said I wanted Chinese. They said they wanted Thai. Mom said it was all the same. "Chinese is not Thai!" I said, and Mom asked, "How come you know the difference when it comes to food?" We ate king cake on our way back to Mississippi. It was creamy and glorious. I got the pink plastic baby Jesus inside and Dad said, "That's great," and Mom asked, "What if she choked on it?"

"It's too wet for Mardi Gras," I say.

Mom says, "The American has spoken. Back to Mississippi for us."

Green is for Mardi Gras beads. Green is for sugar sprinkles on king cake and Saint Patrick's Day in my school. Green is for green onions in pad Thai. I had to pick them out last year.

* * *

THERE IS A big lake in New Orleans called Pontchartrain with little bungalows on sticks. Whenever we drive over it, on a roller coaster type of bridge, I know we'll soon be in Mississippi. The car is warm. Dad is going on about the elections again. Gay marriages won't make a blind bit of difference, blah, blah. Mom is yawning. I know exactly what she will say very soon. She will call out the names of creeks and rivers we pass: Pearl, Wolf, Little Black, Bouie, Hobolochitto, Tallahala, Chunky. Then she will say, "It's terrible. Names are all we ever see of Native Americans."

My parents are predictable. Whenever I say this they laugh, but they are. My mom is for woman power. Everything in the world is her right. Even shopping is her right. In Mississippi, she argues in the mall whenever they ask her to show her ID. "That's discrimination," she'll say. "That is dis-cri-mi-nation." In JC Penney too. At home, she acts like she's the boss of me and Dad. "Eat up." "What's this doing here?" "Can't you flush?" My dad says that's because she is a lecturer. He is a doctor. He gets mad with the president, and still he wants the president to win the elections, to teach the people who are against the president a lesson, because they are not getting it together, especially with health. Every day, when he comes home from work, he yells at the television because of the elections. Whenever the president comes on Mom says, "Ugh, turn him off. That man can't string two words together." Yet she tells me it's not right to be rude to people who can't speak English.

Last election, we voted in school. All my friends voted for the president – before he became president – because the other guy killed babies. "Who said he kills babies?" Mom asked when I told her. "Your teacher? Your friend? What kind of parent says such a horrible thing to their kid? Well, they must have heard it from somewhere. Well, I think grown-ups should keep their political opinions to themselves." I told her I voted for the president. She said, "What! Why?" "Everyone else did," I said. She said, "Listen, I brought you up to stand your ground. To stick up for what you believe in." I said, "Oh, please."

First of all, it was her ground not mine. Number B, I believe in fitting in.

"What's it like being African?" my friend Celeste asked when we used to be friends. "I don't know," I told her. I was protecting my parents. I didn't want Celeste to know the secret about Africans. Bones in meat are very important to them. They suck the bones and it's so frustrating I could cry. My mom is the worst, especially when she eats okra stew. Afterwards she chews the bones to a mush and my dad laughs and asks, "What was that before your teeth got to it? Oxtail? Chicken wings? Red snapper? Crab?" I'm like, get some manners.

Being African was being frustrated again when my teacher showed pictures of clothes from all over the world. When she showed the pictures of Africans, that lame Daniel Dawson asked, "Why are they wearing those funny hats?" and everyone in class laughed.

Green is for the color I like most – yellow. Green is for a color I can't stand – blue. Green is a mixture of blue and yellow. Green is for confusion.

Dad is still talking about the elections. "Where are the weapons of mass destruction?" he asks.

Mom points out of the window and says, "Pearl River."

"You guys," I say. "I have a soccer game tonight."

They start yelling.

"For goodness sake!"

"Again?"

"I don't remember that being in my calendar..."

"Why didn't you tell us before?"

"Soccer is meant for the summer. Only the British play in the spring..."

"Only Americans call football soccer."

My parents are so predictable.

"These people are crazy," Dad says. "The weather is not conducive."

Mom says, "What people? Don't put prejudice in my daughter's heart."

"I didn't mention any race," Dad says.

I'm like, what in the world right now? "You guys," I say. "If you're going to live in this country, you might as well get used to soccer. It's part of life. I'm American. How do you expect me to feel?"

"You know," Dad says. "She's right."

I can't believe he fell for that.

"What time's the game anyway?" Mom asks.

"Six."

"Shit."

"Don't cuss, Mom."

"Sorry, baby, but I hated sports in Africa and I hate them here."

* * *

WE'VE PASSED CHUNKY River. I've finished my book. I think we'll make it in time for my game. Mom asks, "Are you still mad with us?"

"A little," I say.

"Sorry. Today has been a bit. . ."

"I know. Are you happy about your green cards?"

"You have no idea."

"America will soon be number one in the world for soccer," Dad says. "You wait and see. Look at the way they organize themselves. From the grassroots level. Everyone involved."

"Girls too," Mom says, and raises her thumb at me.

I'm not into all that. I know what girls like Celeste can do.

"Even if they don't have any talent," Dad says, rubbing his chin. "They have the money to import talent. Did you hear of that fourteen-year-old? Highest paid in the soccer leagues. Freddy Adu. His family came from Ghana. Immigration will save America."

"Because of soccer?" Mom asks.

Green is for the Comets color. I hope we beat the Comets tonight. I really hope we beat them.

* * *

WE MADE IT to the game. Mom and Dad stayed, maybe because of guilt.

You should see me. My color is red. My number is 00. I'm ready to blast those Comets to kingdom come. I'm dribbling down the field. The lights are like stars. The grass is wet. I have to be careful because Mississippi mud can make you slip and slide. Everyone is cheering, *Come on! Get on it! Get on it!*

I kick that sucker. It zooms like a jet, lands in the corner of the goal post, neat as my bedroom when I get two dollars for cleaning up. Girls on my team are slapping my back, "Way to go! Good one!" My parents are cheering with other parents. This is it. Me, scoring. My mom looking like she loves soccer. My dad looking like he really loves the president. Three of us, looking like we really belong. It's better than finding the baby in king cake, and my team hasn't even won yet.

Niki Aguirre

The Little Man

VERONICA'S EXAGGERATED VOWELS ricocheted through the corridors of the Mesoamerican wing of the Chicago Field Museum.

"Aztec deity believed to be the corn god of fertility. Discovered in a cave in 1942, in the province of Gauna... Guane..."

"Guanimotoana," I said.

"Guanimotoana," she echoed, in the hushed reverent tones of a Discovery Channel presenter during Shark Week.

"No record exists of his name, but researchers have nicknamed him the Little Man."

"I can read too Veronica," I said.

She shrugged. "I like reading out loud. Don't you think I have a good voice?" Forgetting the Corn God for a moment, she turned to me and put her hand to her windpipe to perform her vocal exercises. "*Ah, Eh, Eeh, Oh, Ooh.* See? I've been practicing, Julian."

Veronica was hoping to land an audition for a role as a QVC Model. It had been her childhood dream to work in television, she said. QVC could lead to modelling contracts, toothpaste commercials, maybe even the news someday.

I told her I thought she'd be wasted there; that she had far too much talent to work in a job that made her wear cheap imitation jewellery and smile like a simpleton.

"The Shopping Network is just the tip of the iceberg," she said, "A way to get my foot in the door. Later, I'll move on to better things. I'm still young you know."

In the meantime, Veronica practised her 'craft', by reading aloud to me whenever possible, as if I were an idiot child. I didn't have the heart to point out that her voice wasn't her strongest attribute and her vowels sounded like she had cotton socks stuffed in her mouth. She also had the unfortunate habit of over-emphasising the third or fourth word of every sentence, as if she had grown up watching Captain Kirk on Star Trek.

"I *wonder* why they *call* him the Little Man. Look at his *tiny* hands. See how they're *bunched* up into fists like he is clutching them in rage? Does he *remind* you of anyone Julian?"

I leaned in to get a better look at the glass display that housed the ugly idol made of cornhusk.

The Little Man was so small he seemed to float in the immensity of his tank, like one of those deep-sea divers they have for aquariums. Any other object might have looked lost and vulnerable suspended in empty space, but the tiny deity looked apoplectic, as if he was raging against the unfair confinement of his incarcerated predicament.

"Yes, I can *see* a definite resemblance." Veronica's lips twitched in anticipation, her eyes like green agates glittering in the darkness of the museum; waiting for me to get mad, so she could laugh and accuse me of not having a sense of humour.

"You think you're clever, don't you?" I said.

"Oh *relax*, I'm just teasing."

I was sensitive about my height, I admit it, but recently I felt Veronica had taken on a nastiness that crossed the line of playfulness into the boundaries of playground cruelty. I was deeply humiliated by her idea of a 'joke' and it wasn't the first time. I was crazy about the girl, but sometimes she could be unbearable. Without realising I was imitating the Little Man, my arms were pressed to my body, my fingers knotted together into fists.

I'd invited Veronica to accompany me to the 7th Annual Conference for the Midwest Seed Growers of America. While I didn't plan to attend the entire conference, I had carefully worked out a schedule that allowed me time see the city, network with colleagues and still spend time with her.

Over a late room service breakfast, I sat in my bathrobe spreading cream cheese on a bagel, enjoying one of those rare moments of contentment that doesn't require conversation or synchronized activity; the kind of contentment you get when you've planned well and are at peace with the world. Veronica sat on the corner of the bed, brushing her hair and watching a television programme about cosmetic surgery.

"Do you think I need a boob job?" she asked, cradling her perfect breasts in her hands. "What do you think Jules? Bigger size maybe? You know when gravity decides to take its toll, these *puppies* will be the first to suffer...*hey*, why aren't you paying attention?"

"I told you I hate it when you call me Jules."

"Okay, *Julian*. What are you reading?"

"Just some notes."

"Let me see that... you made a schedule for today? I thought the point of this trip was for us to have a good time together!"

"No. The point of this trip is *work*."

"But you said you weren't going to attend the *stupid* conference. Now you're *changing* your mind? What was the *point* of asking me to come along?"

Not all my time was devoted to Veronica, you understand. Well, not as much as she would have liked. Aside from my regular work, I liked to fashion things out of natural fibres; sculptures, I guess you could call them. I did paintings and drawings as well. Mainly, I liked the feel of mud on my hands: good red country clay instead of plaster. I was experimenting with reeds and grasses lately and was eager to see the Field Museum's Native American artisan display.

"If you were planning to go to museums and stuff, why did you bother to bring me along?" she said in an offended tone, as if I had slighted her on purpose.

Veronica hated it when I mixed business with pleasure.

"I thought you would enjoy seeing some of the sights."

"Fat chance. Can't we do something fun?"

There was that word again. *Fun.* She had been using it against me like a silver bullet, at least a few times a week for the past month.

"It's all *museum* this, architecture that. There's nothing

exciting on here," she said, shoving my itinerary away from her as if it repulsed her.

"Look Veronica, I planned this out carefully. I made sure to include things I thought you would like as well. A little bit of culture won't kill you."

"What are you trying to say?" she said, narrowing her eyes.

"Nothing. Look, let's not fight today."

"You think I need more culture, right?

I remained silent.

"You think I'm not educated like you, that I don't *know* things? Well I know plenty of things. I may not be a la-dee-da artist, but at least I'm not a hick farmer like you."

"I'm not a farmer Veronica, I told you before; I sell organic seeds and supplies to farmers. I'm a *distributor*. Maybe all the hair brushing is affecting your grey cells."

"You can be a real jerk sometimes, you know that *Jules?"* She went back to the mirror to continue the inspection of her breasts. She turned this way and that, huffing like an angry mare, preening and posing and lifting her delicate hoofs.

After a few minutes she calmed down a little and looking over her shoulder to make sure I was watching, she arranged herself into my all-time favourite pose. With her swan neck elongated and her slender back arched, her auburn hair tumbled over her shoulders and fell down to her full buttocks. Strategically positioned near the window, the morning sun bathed her in its golden light so that every inch of Veronica's skin appeared luminous and alive. She could be difficult and extremely vain, but, God, she was beautiful. Better than a classic painting or a Greek statue; she was a heartless Goddess forever trapped in a moment in time.

"Come here darling," I said in a thick voice. "I think I

have something fun we can both do."

It was Veronica's flawless beauty that first captivated me. I was enchanted, then, later, obsessed by the red-haired woman with creamy skin that seemed almost unreal, like something made of wax.

Veronica worked as an artists' model for one of my still life classes. Week after week she sat naked, arms behind her head, legs outstretched on the dais, as we attempted to capture the angles of her limbs, the fleshiness of her curves. She had the uncanny ability to mimic a statue perfectly. The students never ceased to be amazed and delighted by her classical poses, but no one more than I.

As the semester progressed, I purposely began to search her out. I arrived at class earlier and earlier, in hope of catching her doing ordinary things, like eating, or wearing her own street clothes. Did she wear little skirts that showed off the symmetry of her toned legs or long ones that brushed against her taut calves? Did she prefer low-cut tops that hugged her ample assets or faded college sweatshirts? It was strange; I had seen her naked so many times I now fantasized about seeing her clothed.

On the one occasion when I was successful, I watched Veronica wander into the studio eating an apple and wearing a faded pair of blue jeans and a suede jacket. I was so excited; I could barely contain my pleasure. I made a mental note (for later) of how she sat at the back of the empty classroom, reading a magazine and glancing nervously toward the door, as if at any moment the students would march in and find her occupying their space.

I began seeking Veronica out more boldly during classes. I purposely didn't avert my eyes, staring even after she put on her robe and stepped back behind the makeshift dressing room. A few times during her sessions, I thought I noticed her flicking her eyes in my direction, just the smallest shift and then back to her usual statue-like self. I felt a thrill from these brief moments of possibly imagined contact. Often these meagre interactions between us were the highlights of my week.

We carried on this way for some time: me getting crazier and crazier about her with each passing day but too afraid to do anything, until one day, I found her waiting for me after class. Standing outside the classroom door with her hair pulled back, wearing a turtleneck sweater, Veronica, up close and in person, was far better than the frozen goddess of my dreams. I could barely manage a hello, but she smiled and invited me to sit with her over a cup of coffee.

"I hope you don't mind me saying, but you're a little old to be a student," she said.

"Yes, well...I had to work when I was younger. And you know what they say...you're never too old?"

She laughed and told me about all her different jobs: waitressing at a coffee house near the campus, stacking books at the library and working at Kinkos on weekends.

"Wow, why so many?"

"I'm taking a few extra classes: elocution lessons and acting. But what I really want to do more than anything is model. Not for art classes, but you know, for magazines and stuff."

"I'm sure you will get there one day," I said, sipping my cappuccino.

"You think?"

"Absolutely. You are a very striking and beautiful woman. And that's not a pick-up line. I'm being honest. I could see you on the pages of Vogue."

"I'm not tall enough to be a *fashion* model. I'm only 5'9. But I can do commercial modelling. I could sell anything:

automobiles, shampoo, *cereal*... I'd love to model clothes, shoes, makeup and ooooh, rings and *necklaces*. I love *jewellery*," she said. "I heard on some gigs you even get to keep the stuff!"

"Well being tall isn't everything. You have oodles of grace, charisma and poise."

"Thanks. I *like* you Julian. You have a kind face. You remind me a little of *someone* I used to know."

She smiled at me and sipped her black coffee and I smiled right back, but inside my stomach was churning, thinking about who that *someone* was.

After that, Veronica would wait for me on Tuesdays at the café around the corner from the studio. Apart from being incredible looking, she was funny and energetic and her enthusiasm was contagious. Before I knew it, we were engaged in a game of harmless flirting: just a little fun, nothing too serious. But the more time we spent together, the more I noticed our relationship changing. Whenever I would talk to her, she would lean against the diner booth and stretch out like a languid cat until she was almost on my lap. I would carry on of course, pretending she had no affect on me. I thought perhaps she was testing me, waiting to see if I only wanted her for her body and not her mind. On other occasions, she would apply and reapply her cherry flavoured lip-gloss, looking at me and licking her lips the whole time while she was doing it, even though the gloss kept rubbing off on her coffee cup. She traded in her standard jeans for skirts and would sit in front of me crossing and uncrossing her legs as if still wearing jeans. It was enough to make any red-blooded man go wild. I had to constantly remind myself about the dangers of lusting after young women almost half my age. For God's sake, she was only 21!

But some things can't be helped. Veronica drew me the

way the moon draws water and I was helpless, completely besotted when I was around her.

OUR MORNING TOGETHER at the Field Museum was a quiet one. I wasn't sure if that was due to our earlier fight or because the surroundings called for it, but Veronica was particularly reserved, something I attributed to her resentment at being dragged along against her will. I had promised we would do some shopping afterward and she agreed reluctantly, on the condition that we wouldn't spend too much time getting 'cultured' as she called it. We walked through the galleries without speaking or holding hands; only stopping to look at the displays she found interesting. She ignored the Neanderthals, witchdoctors and totem poles. But as we turned the corner at pre-Columbian artefacts, she finally came alive.

"Look at all this gold!"

I smiled like a doting parent. I had a particular passion for the art of the pre-Columbian period myself.

"Imagine wearing all this jewellery."

Her eyes took in the collection of golden bracelets, rings and earrings displayed on the velvet cloth before her. "Look at that," she pointed, *The Necklace of Promises. Worn by the Princess Q'tante on her wedding day."*

I walked up behind her as she leaned over the glass case. The necklace was impossibly heavy – a chain of braided gold links and intricate weavings that resembled an elaborate dog collar. At each end was a clever mechanism of interlinking twists that locked together like a puzzle.

"The Necklace of Promises was designed by the Warrior Prince Tezomoc, for his future bride. The claw clasps at the back, symbolise unity between the two royal families, and the crisscrossing pattern on the chain itself, represents the long road of matrimonial duty and years of bliss that lay ahead for the couple.

As tradition dictated, the necklace was to be put on Q'tante's neck after the wedding, during a private ceremony with the prince. Only he was allowed to put it on or take it off. Once it was on, it was locked for eternity and could never be taken off, even in death."

Imagine having to wear that thing forever?" Veronica shivered.

"A good way to keep your wife under lock and key. Maybe his princess was flighty," I said, spanning my hands around her neck. "Maybe he was afraid she would be unfaithful."

"You don't know that Julian. You only say that because you're not a very trusting person. You don't believe that people can be faithful to one another."

"That's not true."

"Yes it is. Your imagination is pretty limited. You don't even believe in eternal love."

"I'll have you know there's nothing wrong with my imagination. I'm imagining you right now, wearing that necklace and nothing else."

"Stop," she said pushing my hands away.

"Why? Does the thought not excite you?" I bit the tip of her ear.

"Julian cut it out," she said, moving away from me.

Lately she got upset without even needing a reason. She flinched when I tried to touch her and expressed disinterest when I tried to be affectionate. I felt like an ice skater skimming on the thin ice of her indifference. I suppose she had simply grown tired of waiting for me to make a decision and commit to her.

It was true, as she said, that I had issues with trust and commitment, but I was working on changing that. I hadn't told Veronica yet, but I had made reservations at a little

French Bistro downtown. Over a romantic candlelight dinner, I would tell her how much I wanted to spend the rest of my life with her. I would prove to her that I was committed; that I *was* serious.

I had been married once before: a short-lived relationship when I was much younger, little more than a kid really. Aggie was a bookish girl, smart, studious and sweet. We both fell head over heels, but it didn't last and within a year we were divorced. Veronica was different from Aggie; that was certain. She was wilful, more outspoken and had a fearlessness and determination that my first wife lacked completely. With Veronica everything seemed possible. With my ex, everything was precious and tinged with a bittersweet sense of entropy. I tried to remember how crazy I'd been about Aggie, but the memory was remote and distant, like an old sepia photo. It was almost as if it happened to someone else.

I left Veronica gawking at the Necklace of Promises and moved to another display to look at a collection of splendid silver daggers and obsidian knives. One of the daggers had an emerald encrusted handle, with a golden blade. It was elaborately engraved with the face of a beautiful woman who resembled a jaguar. It was a superbly crafted piece of art. The placard said it had belonged to the Warrior Prince Tezomoc. I turned to show Veronica and noticed she was talking to a tall man. He was leaning into her and laughing. He slipped into the shadows as I approached them.

"Who was that?"

"Where?"

"That person I just saw you talking to."

"What are you talking about Julian?"

"The man. I just saw you with a man."

She rolled her eyes at me as if I were crazy. The only man I see here is this guy. Check him out," she said, indicating the icon of Guanimotoana.

The Little Man was directly perpendicular from the Necklace of Promises. But while the necklace was grouped together with shiny artefacts like bracelets, nose rings, toe rings, and headpieces; the minute statue had been tucked in a dark corner where few people would notice it.

"Maybe he's special so he gets a case all by himself," said Veronica, placing her hands on the glass.

For some reason she seemed quite taken with the ugly corn man. From a purely artistic point of view, I found nothing interesting about him. He seemed crude and badly made, especially in the bleak dimness of the funereal lighting.

"He was found buried face first in an unmarked mound," she read in her QVC voice. "It says here...*the Little Man was bound in dark bandages; his turquoise eyes protected by two golden coins."* Veronica took a step back from the display, studying him carefully. "Look at his eyes Julian. They're absolutely breathtaking."

Someone had taken great care with the eyes. Different coloured pieces of turquoise surrounded a larger piece of honey amber. It gave the corn god the disconcerting appearance of having pupils.

"You know what I think? He must have been someone special and that's why he's here all on his alone. Poor little guy must get lonely."

I sighed. Sometimes I forgot just how young she was.

"I wouldn't make any assumptions Veronica. He's probably a common fertility statue."

"No, he's not ordinary: he's *special*. See how he is standing? This little guy was made to be looked at. *I* would know."

I looked at the cornhusk shaped body, the arms akimbo

as if prepared for battle. Despite his ostracised status he didn't look lonely at all. He looked menacing. Although no bigger than a pencil, his diminutiveness didn't in the slightest reduce his haughty, regal demeanour. The hideous little God glared back at us, his ivory teeth shining in the glow of the halogen light. I too would have buried him given the chance.

I showed Veronica a pamphlet I'd picked up about the Little Man.

An archaeologist named Peter Nash discovered him in 1952. Nash wrote a book about the treasures of Xocltalca, which included the Necklace of Promises, the Dagger of Silences and the statue of the Little Man.

Legend had it that the royal priests placed a curse on the necklace after the young princess mortally offended her husband by dying thoughtlessly on their wedding night. Sources had it that before the consummation of the marriage could take place, Prince Tezomoc stabbed his beloved bride in the chest with the engraved dagger with the jaguar's face. Other sources said that the princess was strangled with the Necklace of Promises. Still another story went that the Little Man was actually Tezomoc's brother. He had been Q'tante's lover, but since Tezomoc was the first born, she rightfully belonged to him. The enraged prince finding that the heart of his princess belonged to another, cursed and killed his brother and then his young bride.

Dr. Cassaves, a researcher for the museum, theorised that the Little Man was actually Tezomoc's wrath personified. If you looked closely at the statue, you could see it had a miniature replica dagger on its waist and the patterns of his warrior garbs resembled the curved lines seen on the necklace.

Nash wrote how he found the statue buried under seven layers of dirt, with its eyes heavily bandaged in gauze and facing downward.

The villagers refused to plant their crops near the land where the statue was buried; saying that any animal that sniffed the dirt would grow ill and their crops would be poisoned.

"Don't you think that's fascinating?" I said.

"You know what?" said Veronica. "I'm going to take a picture. I'm going to take a picture of both of you. Why don't you bunch up closer to it and clench your hands."

No sooner were the words out of her mouth, than a man appeared wearing the beige uniform of a Security Guard.

"No pictures please," he said, holding up his hand. "It's against the rules." He gestured to a sign, barely visible in the dim lighting of the Mesoamerican display.

Absolutely no flash bulb lighting or photographic equipment allowed in this wing.

"How did you know I was getting ready to take a photo? Were you following me around?" Veronica raised an eyebrow and the guard flushed a deep red.

"It's my job to keep on eye on things around here, ma'am."

"Well, it's a little hard to see the sign in the dark," she said. "I was just so taken with this little statue. I don't suppose you'd allow me a few quick photos?"

"No Ma'am. I'm afraid that's not possible."

"I understand," she said and pressed her pretty pink lips into a pout.

The guard was tall and muscled, probably in his mid 20s: handsome with blonde hair and a tan. The kind of guy I could imagine Veronica with, if she wasn't with me. The problem with having such a beautiful woman as a girlfriend was that you were never safe from the prying eyes of other men. Like this guy, grinning at her like an idiot. No doubt he had been lurking in the shadows all morning, watching her every move. She seemed to attract the stalker type.

"Excuse me," said Veronica said to the guard, "but don't you think my *friend* here looks a little like the Corn God?"

The guard gave me the once over and furrowed his brow. I had an urge to hit his perfect chiselled chin.

"See the way he is standing?"

I was scowling and had my arms at my waist.

The guard nodded and they laughed. Together. He with his masculine laugh and she with her head thrown back and her long neck exposed to this stupid stranger. Veronica was such a shameless flirt.

"Are you sure I can't take a picture of both of them standing together?" she said, wiping her eyes.

"Oh all right, just a quick one," said the guard. "For you, Princess."

"What did you call her?" I said.

"Don't worry about him, his bark is worse than his bite. *Thank you,* Manny." She gave him her sweetest smile.

When he left, she turned to me and shoved her purse in my hands. "Here hold this", she demanded. Using her mobile phone, she took three shots of the Little Man and me in quick succession.

"Why did you say that to the guard Veronica?"

"What does it matter? It worked didn't it?"

"Well, I wish you would stop comparing me to this thing. It's insulting."

She shrugged and continued taking pictures.

"Listen, we've been here long enough," I said looking at my watch. "Let's go get some lunch."

"No, you go ahead," she said, looking around the room. "I'm not hungry yet. Plus, there a few more things I want to see."

"Like what?"

"I don't know. *Stuff.*"

"I see. So you're going to wait around for your little friend the security guard? Hanging out with him so you can both laugh at me again?"

"Don't be stupid Julian. That was just something I said to distract him. I'm enjoying the museum. That's what you wanted right?"

"Yes, but I can't believe you are wasting time looking at this piece of junk. Especially when you didn't even want to come here in the first place. There are more interesting things to see her, like the Aztec chocolate exhibit. Or the Emperor's collection of crowns, you would love that."

"I don't want to see some stupid chocolate. Besides, I'm not holding you here. If you don't want to be here, leave," she snapped.

"Come on, leave this ugly corn man," I said trying to wrap my arms around her.

She gave me an inscrutable look. "No. You go ahead Julian. I'm going to stay for a bit longer. I need time to think about *things.*"

I finally lost my patience with her.

"Think about things? What is there to think about, Veronica? It is a creepy statue. It was found buried in a cave and it's hideous as well. End of story!" My voice came out louder than I intended. I had been looking forward to walking hand in hand through the dim corridors with her, stopping now and then to kiss on the benches or the alcoves, and here we were fighting.

Manny put his head around the corner. "Mind keeping it down folks? You're disturbing the other patrons."

I glanced around the empty room. We were the only people there.

"Sorry, we'll keep it down."

He winked at my sweetheart and disappeared again.

Veronica turned her back to me and sat on the bench. "What's the big deal?" she whispered.

"What, now you don't want to be with me? Is that it? I don't understand."

"I don't *know,* Julian. I need time to think. Please stop crowding me," she flinched as I tried to grab her hand. "Julian, she said in a low voice. "Why don't you go ahead to the chocolate thing by yourself? I'll meet up with you in a few hours. Let's meet at that tea room place you said."

"But I thought…"

"Please! I just want to be on my own for a few hours." And with that she looked around the room again and took off in the other direction, leaving me standing in the gallery alone.

For the third time that day she had succeeded in belittling me. I clenched my fists together and felt the bile in my throat. I vowed it would be the last time.

THE CHOCOLATE EXHIBIT turned out to be a big let down. In fact, the rest of the museum seemed as dead as all its exhibits without Veronica's company. On my way out, I noticed a gift shop.

"Excuse me," I said to the pretty blonde woman behind the counter.

"May I help you sir?"

"This necklace, is it an exact replica of the Necklace of Promises?

"Yes," said the woman, "Would you like to see it?" She lifted it out of its velvet case. "A beautiful handmade piece. See the elaborate workmanship on the gold? Just like the original. Are you a collector?"

"No, it's a gift," I said… A gift for my *wife.*"

"Isn't she the lucky lady," said the blonde.

"I'm the lucky one."

"How *romantic.* I wish my boyfriend who hurry up and propose already." Her laugh had a little tinkle.

"Do you really think she will like it, *Anne?*" I said, leaning in and reading her nametag.

Anne blushed as if I had asked her to meet me in my hotel room. "It's absolutely gorgeous."

I SAT IN the Russian Tea Room, fingering the package the shop assistant had thoughtfully tied with red ribbon. Veronica was going to be so excited when she saw it. I imagined her opening the lid, delighted and breathless like a little girl. She would demand that I clasp the necklace to her beautiful neck. I would lift the hair off the back of her neck and lean in and inhale her wonderful musky smell. The smell I had often told her she could bottle and sell, if the television thing didn't pan out.

For a brief moment, I even considered what it would be like if I gave her the Necklace of Promises as a wedding present. I could almost see the soft tears rolling down her lovely face. Her happy look of utter devotion and love was priceless.

The first time we slept together, Veronica confessed how she'd developed a little 'crush' on me in the art classes. She could see me concentrating as I looked at her naked body and the thought excited her so much, she had to force herself to sit still. She said she noticed the delicate movement of my hands as they sketched her and it turned her on.

"I found you so attractive, so irresistible even, it drove me crazy. But I couldn't do anything about it as approaching people from the class could get me fired. One day I came in early to see if you were around. I saw you then, looking at me as if you thought I was the best thing in the world and I knew you felt the same way."

She told me she wasn't in the habit of flirting with male students, in case I had the wrong idea about her. Then she turned away from me and said that sometimes when she caught my eye she wondered what I was like. Was I kind? Was I romantic? Was I involved with anyone else? I didn't wear a wedding ring, but perhaps there was a girlfriend. And with this last comment she placed her small hand on top of my chest. I felt my skin burn beneath her hand, as if seared by the radiance of her touch. I didn't say a word, afraid she would remove it and with it my heart.

Then Veronica said it was inappropriate for us to have any kind of relationship. I was too old for her and she was a girl who liked to go out and have a good time. She wasn't ready for a serious relationship. As I leaned over to touch her hair and tell her I understood everything, I noticed she was crying. I pressed my lips lightly to hers to soothe her and then next thing you know, I was holding her so tightly she could hardly breathe. Veronica brought something primal out of me. In her arms I discovered what had been missing from my life all those years, even when I was with Aggie. I finally knew what it was to love someone with a fierce and devoted passion and now that I found her, I was never going to let go.

An hour and forty-five minutes later, I was still waiting for Veronica at the restaurant. I glanced at my watch again. I noticed the waiter hovering discreetly with a pitcher of water. I called him over and ordered another whisky.

"Will you be having anything to eat sir?"

I shook my head brusquely and he took the menus away.

My appetite was now completely spoiled and I was

starting to get a migraine. I reached into my jacket and touched the pretty box with the necklace. I liked the sensation of the fragile paper against my fingers. It felt even better to crush it in my hand until I felt it tear and crumble. I poured the amber liquid down my throat in one smooth gulp and ordered another one.

I didn't see Veronica again until much later, back at the hotel. I came out of the shower to find her sitting on the bed. "Where were you today," I said, trying to keep my voice even.

"I was at the museum."

"All this time?"

"Yes. I told you I had a few things to think about."

"So you said. Veronica, is there something you want to tell me?" I said putting on a clean shirt.

"Now is not the time Julian. I'm not feeling very well"

Concern overtook my anger. "What's wrong, my love?" I said, coming over to her and taking her hand. Perhaps it was my imagination but I noticed an odd smell on her: a combination of cigar smoke, drink and something else I couldn't place. "So all this time you've been in the museum?" I asked.

"Let go of my hand Julian, you're hurting me,"

"Why don't you tell me the truth then? What were you really doing?"

"What? Are you crazy? I TOLD you. I was in the museum. Jesus, Julian. Why are you staring at me like that?"

"No reason," I said, behind gritted teeth. I released her arm and she headed for the bathroom without another word.

When she emerged a half hour or so later, her eyes and nose were pink. That's the bad thing about redheads; their colouring is so extreme. Any sort of blush or blotch shows up drastically in their pigment.

She was wearing a bathrobe and her hair was wrapped in a towel. She sat on the chair near the bed and began to put on her make-up.

"You should really wear your hair up tonight," I said coming up behind her. "You look gorgeous when you do. It enhances your beautiful, elegant neck."

"I like it down," she said dotting foundation on her cheeks.

"I bought you something today."

"Oh?" she said, still applying her make-up, not meeting my eye in the mirror.

I reached into my jacket pocket and pulled out the rumpled package and handed it to her.

"Why is it all torn up?" she frowned.

"I dropped it and someone trampled on it," I lied, unable to tell her I had mangled it myself while waiting for her to show up at the restaurant.

I could barely contain myself as she slowly took the box from me, tore off the paper, and flipped open the case. Unlike my earlier fantasies, Veronica just stared at the necklace.

"It's like the one in the museum," I said, my voice unnatural. "Like the one of Princess whatshername."

"I know, Julian. I can't believe you bought me a necklace that was cursed." She spun toward me, a small flame ignited in her eyes.

"What are you talking about?"

"Cursed, yes. Don't you remember? The prince cursed his wife when he accused her of sleeping with someone else."

"That's a legend, Veronica. A *myth*. Is that what you spent all day doing? Listening to that stupid guard with the cleft in his chin telling you stories?"

"Why would you say that? I *read it myself* Julian. I'm not STUPID. I *can* read you know. God, I was standing beside you! Don't you remember?"

I was feeling dizzy, so I sat on the bed and put my head between my knees. "I saw you admiring the necklace, I thought you would like it," I said in a low voice.

She was shaking now; the tears falling slowly down her face, streaking her makeup. "You don't understand. There isn't anything wrong with the present. It's us Julian; *we* are all wrong. I've tried to do everything possible to make it work. We're just too different. I told you from the start. I'm too young to get involved. You told me you didn't want anything serious, but now it seems you want more. I can't give you that. I can't accept your gift. I'm sorry." She put the necklace in my hand.

I have only cried three times in my life. The first time was when my mother died.

The second time was when Aggie told me she was leaving. The third time was now.

Veronica looked away, ashamed for me, or for herself. I was sure this was not the first time she had broken some poor fool's heart. Despite her tears, she seemed to be enjoying it. Since the start of our relationship when she was flirting with me at the diner, I knew she was capable of anything, but I was weak and couldn't help myself. I bit the inside of my lip until it bled and forced myself to stop crying.

"I understand," I said to her in a raspy voice. "I understand how a young girl like you would feel trapped and suffocated in a relationship with a divorced man,"

"It's not you, it's me," she said using the standard break up line. The bitch had the audacity to look sad.

"Can I ask you a favour," I said in such a low pathetic voice so she had to lean over to hear me. "Please do me the honour of going out with me tonight. Just one final time." I noticed she was about to object but I pressed on. "Just for tonight. As *friends*. After that you're free to go. I can sleep on the sofa bed tonight, and tomorrow we'll go our separate ways. I can't deny how I feel about you Veronica. It will be hard but I'll do the right thing and let you go," I allowed my voice to break.

She sat thinking about it for a few minutes and then nodded at me.

"One more thing. I took the velvet case and pulled out the necklace. "Will you wear it? It was made for a princess and I can't think of anyone who would look lovelier wearing it."

She was after all a stupid, stupid little egotistical girl. She deserved all that she got threefold.

I walked behind her and she collected the strands of hair off her neck, just as I had imagined it. I reached over and clasped it tightly around her throat. It was a perfect fit. I thought of her perfect, elegant neck, the very neck that I loved so much and that would be denied to me after this night and the pang of loneliness hit me so hard, I almost burst into tears again. Inwardly I cursed Veronica to the deepest realms of hell.

"That's too tight Julian," she said, as I leaned in to suck up as much of her wonderful scent as I could. Except, I couldn't smell her natural odour, not with the cigar smoke and male cologne and all the other shit in her hair.

"Shhh, just sit still," I said as I triggered the secret link that latched it together. There. Now don't you look stunning?"

I brought over a hand mirror so she could admire herself.

Over dinner Veronica sat very quietly, hardly saying a word the entire evening. At one point I turned to her and forgetting myself, I reached out for her hand. It was like a dead bird.

I whispered in her ear, "Are you alright, my love? You look a little pale."

Her breath was very agitated.

"The necklace looks beautiful on you," I said. "I could see why the Prince chose it for his bride."

"Yeah? Well it's the most uncomfortable thing ever. It feel like thorns inside my neck."

"Well, it looks lovely."

"I'm sorry. I should have told you how I was feeling Julian. I hate the way things have turned out between us."

"Is there someone else? Can you at least tell me that?"

"Julian… I thought we weren't going to…"

"Well? Is it a yes or a no?"

"I can't believe this…"

"Relax Veronica. Please sit down. I won't mention it again."

I knew it. I knew the conniving bitch had someone on the side. I suspected it weeks ago, when I went to pick her up after class and she was late. When she arrived her cheeks were flushed and I mentioned it, joked that she must have been flirting with someone and she froze.

"I've had enough, Julian. I'm tired and I just want to take this thing off and go back to the hotel."

So now she was too tired to be with me. I bet she wasn't too tired to be with someone else, doing something *fun*, no doubt.

I noticed angry blotches appearing underneath her neck where the necklace was rubbing against her skin.

"Fine," I said. "Let's go back."

As soon as we got to the hotel she started undressing. "Help me take it off," she said, her hands struggling with the clasp. "Can you help me with this? It feels like it's pressing against my throat."

"Veronica, it's just a necklace."

She was getting upset now. "I can't get this damn thing off!" She fumbled futilely with the necklace, "Julian don't just stand there! Help me take it off."

"Stop struggling and let me see what I can do," I stood behind her trying to unclip the brooch the way the blonde woman had demonstrated. It refused to unlock.

"Oh my God, what did you do?"

"Nothing, nothing at all. Why would you think I did something?"

"It's pressing against my windpipe," she turned toward me and started to panic a little. Her face went a strange colour. "Julian, I can't breathe! It's cutting off my air supply."

"Veronica, please stand still. I can't help you if you're thrashing around."

She was gasping and coughing, making low moaning sounds and yanking at her neck.

"Veronica! Stop moving!" My arms were struggling with the necklace but it seemed to get more tangled with any effort to get it off her neck.

Things happened very quickly then.

I remember Veronica clutching at her throat, her eyes bulging as if the necklace were a tourniquet. I remember her face going pale and her arms feeling like cold marble against mine as she wrestled with the latch.

She cried and pleaded for me to help her, dripping

spit, snot and tears on the lapels of my suit. I was highly disgusted.

And then she passed out.

When she awoke a few minutes later, I had removed her dress and had her stretched out on the bed: naked but still wearing the necklace.

Her hands flew to her throat. She cried out on finding it still around her neck.

"Calm down Veronica."

She began to thrash around again.

"Listen, it seems to tighten the more you move around, so stay still."

She screamed then. A horrible piercing sound like a wounded animal.

I slapped her. Harder than I wanted, but it felt good to feel her skin connect with my hand. Afterward, she was quieter, propped on the pillows, her eyes gazing at nothing in particular.

"I'm sorry I can't take off the necklace. You know that only true love can release you from its captivity. I guess you don't have much of a choice. You can either learn to love me again or you can keep that fucking necklace around your neck for the rest of your life. There, there," I said, stroking her beautiful hair as she sobbed. "Everything is going to be alright."

T. TARA TURK

A Cigarette

HE'D LEFT A note saying that he was going to come back. That he needed air. Something about windows not working around there, didn't she pay the bill for the AC man, was it stuffy and how come she wasn't hot like he was. She didn't answer. It was as if he forgot how much in love they'd been once and how sometimes that makes you not have to say anything about anything and why he was wasting time with these words that kept dogging her as she changed the baby's diaper and picked up little Sam's toys from under both of their feet, she couldn't really understand.

They had a neighbour down the hall who would later say that he heard him stomping past his apartment like there was a fire so he had to look out the peep hole and that's when he saw the bag he was carrying like he was going on a trip. Didn't she see? She would shake her head no. At that moment she was sitting on the couch, crappy TV blaring some kid's show that she could never remember the name of but was happy it existed because the kids were quiet when the magic lights came out of the box. The smell of bacon still hung to the couch and the walls from breakfast earlier that morning. She hadn't opened the shades yet but there was yellow, murky light peeping through letting her know there was a day going on and she should get ready for it. But she couldn't. The pit in her stomach was too big and it scared her and it had voices making her remember all of her childhood nightmares of "he's going to leave you." The baby has a scratch on her lid and crusties in her eye. Sam needs to blow his nose. They all need air.

One and a half years ago prior to her sitting on this coach and not being able to move because of the sheer weight of someone leaving you at the precise moment they shouldn't, she was in the streets. She was living next to a dumpster. She was in love with a man who promised to take care of her, only that meant him getting them food to eat or twenty dollars in change from standing outside of the supermarket in the parking lot next to the fresh flowers. She had been filthy with matted hair and was about to learn that she was three months pregnant. It had begun with him saying she was the most beautiful woman he'd ever met. Right when credit card debt was piling up but was the last of her worries, when disconnect notices meant it's finally time to pay the bill, when she called no money "creative accounting." She had her own place once but it was a dive that was so crooked things would roll from one side of the apartment to the other. There was a musty water smell enclosed in the chipping paint and partial wallpaper on the walls. She vacuumed everyday but to no avail because things always seemed to be on the carpet.

She would sit there and wish for better, wait for

opportunity or chance to ring the doorbell and take her out for a beer or a meal or a kind word. She waited with TV dinners in front of her, with cigarettes burning (cigarettes oh cigarettes where are you now??), with old love songs playing. She would just wait.

HE CAME ALONG and told her that smoking was bad as she waited for the bus one day and he was walking by going someplace that looked important because his shoes, well his shoes were clean and shiny and didn't have scuffs on them. He didn't mind her mismatched set of gloves or the fact that she was wearing a coat from ten years ago or that she was really a very striking woman. He didn't like the cigarette dangling from her mouth. Let's talk about it over dinner one day, he said. She was so in shock, she had nothing to say. She just nodded. That's what happens when you are alone and you have no one, when family won't remember that you exist, when friends are leery of you because bad luck seems to follow you and they think it's contagious. That's what happens when you don't use your voice any more. You loose it.

But he gave it back to her. Gave her laughs and good times. Gave her the first Indian dinner she had and she remembered saying to him "Oh it's spicy like my Aunt Kimmel's food" and he said "Kimmel? What the fuck is a Kimmel??" and from that point on she was in love because Aunt Kimmel had always said she would be up to no good in her life and how could he know that. He had a twinkle in his shifty eye. She liked the twinkle, discarded the shifty and fell in love.

IT STARTED WITH a toothbrush left. A sock under the bed. Underwear left in her hamper to wash. Coats not needed for that spring day so left in the closet. Soon he followed all of his things and didn't leave. And the money he spent on her for dinner didn't reappear come bill time. He would just make arrangements with her. "Say uh baby, you pay that and then I'mma hit you off next week when this thing comes through I got goin. Then we really gonna eat good and get outta here. Let me get a five."

Before she had enough to stretch around her own life, almost. Creative accountant that she was, she always had debt but was one step away from being carted off, reported or evicted. But her money didn't stretch around two people at all. TV dinners disappear faster. No more cigarettes (he'd decided to not touch her if she smoked and of course one addiction goes to another – she was addicted to his touch now, loving the metallic taste of his fingers and the roughness of his heels rubbing against her calves in bed). They fell behind. And behind.

She'd never seen an eviction notice before. Didn't know what they looked like. Heard that it took a long time to actually get you out but it didn't seem like a long time when they were in a shelter, then in front of his sister's house (she didn't answer) then another shelter, a friend's couch (the friend liked to touch her), then the street (he'd broken his friend with the couch's jaw when he found out). The street has so many crevices but no room for anything she'd ever had. All of that was in a pawn shop and she left knowing she'd never see it again but that was okay because his hand was on her lower back when they gave it to the man behind the bullet proof counter who inspected her TV, her stereo, her first gold necklace. It was fine because he was tall and shielding her from the badness of the world, the cold wind that wrapped around them as they walked the streets, which is what they did most days. Because you can't be homeless and have a job. You can't keep a job if they find you sleeping in conference rooms and washing up in the bathroom. Especially if your amour is with you. They ask you both to leave. And you leave. And then you have nothing to stretch anymore.

THEY SAW THINGS together. They saw birds in the park and people fucking behind trees with a desperate hunger that she felt for a bed, a meal or a cigarette. He wanted to take her behind a tree when they saw people fucking but she would never let him. He would get mad at her because she never let him touch her anymore, because he knew that she blamed him for not taking care of business like he said. But he would never say that. He would look into her brown eyes that were now surrounded in red veins and say it was her fault that should couldn't do her end to take care of them. They were a "them." She tried to remember when that happened. A sock. A toothbrush. Underwear left in a hamper. Someone saw them argue in the park and she saw them through that person's eyes, just by the way they looked at her. They saw them as that kind of crazed delusional homeless couple that sounds like that they argue about people who aren't there or beer money or stealing their drugs. They were not on drugs. She thought.

HE LIKED EVERYTHING. He liked her smile, though crooked in some areas. He liked her skin though getting patchy because they couldn't wash everyday. Her eyelashes. Her smell. The way his drugs tasted on her fingers. This was new. This happened next to a dumpster when she was three months pregnant and didn't know what do. Happy, partially, because they never had money for tampons or pads so she didn't have to steal or be soiled. Sad for all the obvious reasons. He was sniffing off of her finger. And she said it. "It's gonna be a baby." He got up and took a piss behind the dumpster. He walked down the alley and pulled at himself, angry. Not at her. Crying. It was like a cry of grief of mourning. He touched the brick walls that had boxes piled high and knocked them all down. Someone came out threatening to call the police. He looked at her. And she realized that he just might love her.

He'd gotten himself arrested so she could have a better chance of staying in a shelter since they don't take full families at most of them. Like the man is supposed to be out working and he doesn't need a place to put his head at night. So he robbed a store, gave her the money and made her leave, and sat down on the curb waiting for the police to come. He only got some months and probation. But by that time the shelter had given her this place and the welfare kicked in and they had little Sam and then love got big between them when he went out looking for a job in the day and told her, at night under the covers in the dark where it was safe that he had never been one to be responsible but this time he needed to because they were his life now and it needed to be straight for once after years of taking detours and short cuts. He grabbed her breasts as her back pressed against him and they listened to Sam breathing on the twin mattress next to their bed and he said, "I am trying for real, baby." And she believed him. It sounded so earnest, so sincere and isn't that more important than succeeding sometimes? She told herself yes, yes it was more important. And then she felt it. The IT she felt when Sam was conceived. And she was right. There was another one.

This time he didn't pull at himself or do a mournful cry. This time he looked at her blankly. This time he went to the murky shades and touched the bookcase and felt dust. And he'd been out all day, working on cars. Being berated by the owners. Trying. Adding metal to his fingers. Wanting a hit but remembering rehab in prison. Counting the twelve steps, wanting to find a new program, being on a waiting list. Seeing bills on the table. Her. Having babies like they cost nothing. He was trying. There was a snap in his back. He didn't know where it came from. Nothing hurt though. Just a snap. A decision maybe. Everything else was mechanic. Like him.

MONTHS OF BEING big. Of having a baby already. Of wanting
to get another job but knowing no one hires a pregnant
woman. Months of making a bed with worn sheets. Of
accepting tea and oatmeal from the nice man next door for
breakfast. She likes talking to him more. He tells her good
things. Things to read. Gives her books. Says he's a social
worker. She listens to his stories. He talks about homeless
people he works with. Talks about one day wanting to quit
because there's no money but seeing a couple in the park
argue, homeless. And how he thought to himself, they need
someone to reach out to them. Someone to turn a light on
since their world seems so dark. How the man flailed his
arms and pulled at himself and knocked boxes down. How
the woman sat there in a ball, curled, a lump of old clothing
and tears. And she knows immediately that it was she and
him. But she says nothing.

He likes walking home from work. He is smiling because
the guys at work are funny. Good to him. Like a family
almost. Order him sandwiches when times are hard for
lunch. Ask him to come out with them and have some fun
but he says, no, new baby and what not on the way. . .But
they understand. Another time. One of them is crashing
on another's couch cause his old lady threw him out. That's
what men do, they say, take care of each other. Like they
take care of the cars. He has never smiled without motive.
These men and these cars make him smile. The men are
men he's never seen before, never had around. He likes cars
because they hum and that's all you hear. Children scream.
They are cute and connected to him but they scream. And
mates, well, they look at you, waiting. Nothing to say.
Large, adding things to themselves you can't quite place.
Don't know what she says half the time anymore. Why can't
he fit into this mold? The air is clean. A pretty woman at
the bus stop looks at him and smiles. He can't remember
the last time that's happened. Maybe she will turn him
off automatic. Make everything fleshy again. He keeps

walking. And walking. Turns around when he realizes he past the apartment. Realizes that he liked passing it.

BABY GIRL BORN seven pounds no complications but doesn't cry when she comes out of her mother's womb. Nobody really there to scream and holler and say "congratulations she looks just like you!" Just two silent people staring at each other, in a look of relief over another hump. Another milestone reached. The social worker down the hall leaves her a basket at the door when she comes home. Diapers and formula and stuff. She is now in a house with two children. The air is thick. They are wonderful. The air is thick. It misses something. Then one day it happens. The social worker man offers her a cigarette after one of his long hard days (he only smokes sometimes and knows it's not good but what's one vice, right?). They smoke and talk about the news as he makes her tea. She chokes on the cigarette. So nasty. She looks at him. It is good though. It is very good.

He smells it on her breath. On her clothes when he comes home after circling the block five times. He looks at her as though this was the last betrayal. First the kids, then the silence and now this. She doesn't even seem to really mind. Her body hasn't been touched in so long. Connection lost maybe. He asks her about the heat in the room, so hot, the bills on the table, he is trying to get someplace in his dialogue with her but is off track. She looks at him brazen and tells him the babies need baths. She takes them in the bathroom and shuts the door. Shuts him out. He is not part of that part of the routine. He is left alone in the living room. Cigarette smoke smell lingering, mixing with bacon smells. He sees books around that she's reading. He has never noticed them before. He rubs his tired face, hot like chocolate, maybe expecting a portion of it to be in his hands. He writes a note. He wants to try this new feeling. This new addiction of going past his home. He has a bag packed in minutes. He sits on the couch and looks at his home. He sits on a chair and looks at his home. He sits at the kitchen table and looks at his home. At no angle does he see himself in it. He walks out. Stomping.

AND SHE IS here now, murky light peeking through, babies clean but snot always around. She sits with her legs open, mouth open, eyes open, what is pouring out of her? There is a relief. She is afraid to say that. A relief. A hand no longer pressing on her spine. No body shielding her from the world because they are so tall and so overbearing. Wouldn't ever let her leave. Tried to make his home nice. She takes the babies and they walk down the hall. Every step brings her closer to her desire. Crazy but it's true. Every step liberates her from this track she's on that she can't get off of. She thinks of it. How glorious it is. How weird it is to get back into it. She knows it will take time and she has that. Tomorrow other things start. Jobs. Schools. She has hit rock bottom and now knows how strong she could be. But today, today she is getting back into the swing of things. He answers. Let's her in. And she takes a cigarette.

If music be the food of love, play on:
Give me excess of it, that, surfeiting,
The appetite may sicken and so die.
That strain again! It had a dying fall;

– William Shakespeare, "Twelfth Night"

KEN NASH

The Cello Garden

THE VIOLINS WERE coming up nicely and the basses had just begun to sprout. The French horns already were in full bloom and the timbales were looking very robust. There was a promising row of bassoons this year (thank God, after meager harvests the last two years) and I was rather proud of my piccolos and flutes. Many times in the past I'd won competitions for both – blue ribbons, nonetheless – and it looked like this year's crop would be unfailing. What concerned me, though, were the cellos.

I had watered thoroughly – not too much – and applied plenty of manure, but the cellos were just not growing. They hadn't even broken through the loose, well-tilled soil. I checked to make sure the seeds had not been stolen by birds or, perhaps, a rival orchestral gardener, but they were all still in place, nestled silently within the procreant earth. They just refused to grow, crack out of their embryonic carapace and reach upward toward air and light. My cellos were being stubborn this year and I was not sure why. In all my years as a gardener of orchestras, a conductor of acoustic agronomy, nothing like this had ever happened. The worst had been those two years of meager bassoon growth I mentioned. But for an entire cello section to refuse to grow – this was quite puzzling.

I began consulting manuals, almanacs, compositions and compendiums. I studied the notes left behind by Beethoven and Bach, Mozart and Mendelssohn, to see if any of these great symphonic harvesters had come across similar incidents. But I found nothing helpful. The cello, it seems, had always been a reliable instrument, a hardy, prodigious instrument. Some even called it the zucchini of orchestral vegetation. I finally put the books aside and went to see my friend Irving.

IRVING LEIBOWITZ, A Russian immigrant Jew. A virtuoso with string vegetation, of course. All those Russian Jews were practically born with a bow-stem in their hands. It was Irving who had provided the seeds – brought over from the Ukraine – for my basses, my violas, my violins, and my cellos.

Irving lived in an apartment complex on the west side of town. He'd grown partially deaf and his fingers were hooked and stiff from rheumatism. He received Social Security from the government and a small pension from the city orchestra, where he played violin for twenty-three years. He had lived in this apartment of his for the past fifteen years, moving here from his house in Treble Park shortly after the death of his wife Inanna, or Anna, as she was known.

I tried to visit whenever I could but orchestral gardening is a full-time job. There were also my students at the university to attend to. And, in order to stay in the good graces of the widowed dean, I was giving her hopelessly inept daughter, Chloe, private violin tutelage twice weekly. At best, I saw Irving perhaps once every three months. Usually I would find him sitting in silence, his tabby cat, Stradivarius, seated on his lap, his hooked fingers steadily stroking Strad's speckled fur.

On this visit, however, Irving was up and slowly moving around the apartment with a watering can in hand. He had a little pot of harmonicas growing beside the sofa and a window box full of penny whistles. On the fireplace mantel was a vase of freshly cut recorders set beside a photograph of Anna when she was a young woman, when she had first arrived in America.

THOSE HAD BEEN heady days for Irving and Anna. He liked to reminisce with me about them and I was always happy to hear stories about that period in American life when the streets were alive and mellifluous with the sounds of many nations, when the young men from Europe were eager to start careers and families in America, "The New World," as Dvorak had dubbed it. Irving arrived with his new bride, a pocket full of seeds and hope for a better life.

"NATHANIEL," IRVING GREETED me, setting his watering can beside the open door. He took my hand with his stiff fingers and led me into the apartment. "Glad to see you today. Today is a special day for Stradivarius and myself. It's the anniversary of my marriage to Anna." There was a weighty photo album on the coffee table that he'd pulled out for the occasion. He showed me pictures of their early years together in America. There was a photo of Anna and him seated with Irving Berlin. Another of them both walking down West Avenue with a young Arthur Fiedler. One of Anna planting a kiss on Benny Goodman's forehead. He pointed out a nightclub photo of Louis Armstrong, cheeks puffed out, blowing a trumpet.

"That's one of mine," he said, full of pride. "I grew it just for Sachmo." I was impressed, having thought of Irving all these years as being principally a gardener of string quartets. "My heart is with the strings," he told me, "but I had a bit of a brass thumb, too, in those early years, and grew some fine, fine trumpets and trombones. Much later in life I began to concentrate solely on the strings. I was experimenting even back then, crossbreeding violas and harps, basses and lyres. From those early experiments I developed my first theories of dominant versus recessive acoustics." I had read many of his articles published in the Music Harvesters Almanac and other periodicals, and was familiar with a number of his theories. He was a true musical pioneer, the Gregor Mendel of musicology.

After hearing his remembrances for a while, and imbibing a hearty glass of *slivovic* or two, I brought up the subject of my cellos, how they were not coming up this year. Irving averted his eyes, shrugged his shoulders and said, "It may be nothing; just give them more time." He got up from the sofa and moved toward the door where he'd left his watering can. "Listen, Nate," he said, carrying the can into the kitchen, "if they don't take I'll compensate you for the loss as best I can." This was a ridiculous statement for him to make since I knew Irving had little money, that he was just scraping by. But Irving felt a certain obligation in the matter since it was he who had given me the seeds for this year's cello crop, as he had done every year previously. In late March, the seeds were handed over without a word that any change had been made. But now, confronted about it in his own apartment, Irving confessed that he had given me a new strain of seeds that he believed might improve upon previous harvests.

I had my doubts, but what was I to do? I let the issue

drop and decided to wait a few more weeks, see what emerges from my garden.

WE HAD PERHAPS the worst storm I remember in many years. It was marvelous and horrific all at once, like a Wagner symphony. Thunder rumbled and crashed like mammoth cymbals. Lighting shot down from the tenebrous sky. The whole town trembled and the powerlines burst open in live-wire sparks. Many homes had been damaged in the storm. Two had caught fire and burned completely to the ground. A dozen or so people had been injured and three had died in accidents said to be related to the storm. One had been a neighbor of mine, Mrs. DaCapo, an elderly patron of the arts who'd come to her untimely end when the Steinway grand she was hiding beneath collapsed.

I went outside the morning after the storm to clear fallen branches and check the house for damage. There was nothing much to speak of, a few loose roof cymbals and a fallen trellis of piano keys. I wandered out back to the garden, a bit panicked over what I might find. I was relieved, though, to see that my garden had remained pretty well intact, except for a couple of partially uprooted xylophones.

Then I saw the row where I'd planted the cellos. There were sprouts! At last! I was overjoyed and relieved, and I began looking forward, at last, to the fall when I would have a complete orchestra growing in my garden, perhaps my finest ever.

THINGS DID NOT turn out exactly as planned. But, like any good gardener, I try to make allowances for the unexpected. The trouble was with my cellos still. They had begun to grow – oh yes – but not quite in the way my previous cellos had come up. They were thin, nearly flat. I tapped on one and heard just a dull melonous thump, instead of the hollow ring I had expected. I feared that this year's entire cello crop would have to be turned to mulch.

I blamed Irving and I was angry. *He had switched seeds on me! Experimenting!* when he, himself, knew that so much rested upon my garden, that I could ill afford to take such risks. And now it was certainly far too late in the year to replant. My fall orchestral season would be ruined without my cello section and Irving was solely responsible.

I avoided confrontation for some time. I did not call or visit Irving all summer. Then unexpectedly, Irving, who rarely makes phone calls, rang me. Perhaps he knew already about the cello business, because his voice did sound a bit hesitant, full of sheepish culpability.

"Nate, my friend, how are things? Well, I hope. And the garden? Is everything coming up alright?"

I could not contain my anger, especially after having just come from the garden where I saw, plain as day, the cellos sprouting baroque flourishes of thorny vines, their rotund shells dull and pitted with abrasions. They looked entirely unplayable.

"Irving, I can't believe you would do this to me. I've been your friend for so long. I always trusted and admired you. But you – you know how important my garden is to me. A whole season of Mendelssohn and Dvorak and Tchaikovsky and Vivaldi is scheduled. Advanced season tickets already sold. And here you give me these 'seeds', these impossible seeds that have totally thrown off the stability of my harvest. Irving, why would you do a cheap thing like this to a friend?" Oh, I was angry. I wasn't even interested in whatever flimsy explanation Irving might have offered. I just wanted to vent an entire spring and summer's worth of fury and frustration into the plastic receiver of my phone.

"I know you can't afford to reimburse me for my cellos,

Irving. There really isn't any possible way to repair the damage done. The best I can hope is that City College over-watered again this year and the Philharmonic's *Carmen* gets overrun by gypsy moth. Oh, this is a mess. The worst mess I've been in in all my years. Not a single cello worth a damn. I might as well just pull out the whole damn lot and turn them to compost."

"No, don't!" Irving shouted. He had said not a word during my tirade, listening stoically to it all, but suddenly his voice cried in panic. Pleading with me, he continued, "Nathan, please don't. Promise me you won't pull out the cellos before they've ripened. I'll do what I can later to make it up to you, but just do me this one favor and let them be."

My anger subsided beneath his desperate pleas. I reminded myself of all that Irving had done for me over the years, the seeds and the good advice. His intentions had never been malicious though, I confess, there was a time when such subterfuge would not have been entirely unexpected. You see, I alone perhaps had more to do with the death of his wife, Anna, than any other person.

LET ME EXPLAIN a thing or two about Anna, first, before I say much more. I had never met Anna Leibowitz, but had seen her play on occasion. She was a gifted cellist – there's no denying that – but in my opinion she'd made some dreadful choices; she took a beautiful, refined instrument and turned it into a thing of horror, of mutated sound and discordant, a-rhythmic – well, *noise*, really.

I was fresh out of the conservatory and becoming known for my astute concert and phono-graft reviews. I had several pieces already published in Music Harvesters Almanac, as well as the Agro-Audio Review and Instruments Digest. When Music Harvesters asked me to do a review of an Anna Leibowitz solo performance, I leapt at the chance, especially knowing she'd spent the previous two years in seclusion working on what was supposed to be the crescendo of her career, a performance of her own composition titled "Eleusis: The Unspeakable Mysteries."

Mind you, all this was well before I'd ever met Irving, though I was well aware of his work and of how he had left the symphony to dedicate himself entirely to pure research and theory. Well, in short, *The Unspeakable Mysteries* turned out to be *unlistenable*, as well. Half the audience left even before intermission. I stayed only because I had a review to write, though I must confess I stopped paying attention at some point. The jumble of shifting Phrygian scales and tumultuous double stopping vanquished all lyricism. The percussiveness of her erratic *col legno* bowing dented and contorted all tempo. The animal-like screeches that reverberated from the cello's corpus – well, they gave me chills of horror. I was frightened by the brutality, the violence of her music, its carnality. Such playing was a tense, sustained, neck-breaking game where art danced self-destructively along the rim of impossibility. God knows what she was trying to prove up there, but in a single performance she had destroyed what, until then, had been an impeccable and admirable career.

It is true my review was a bit harsh, giving no mention of her technical mastery or of her sheer physical endurance. Nor even of some of the more innovative tonalities and techniques, which a few contemporary performers have recently begun to adopt. But I was young and full of brass and truly aghast at what she had subjected her audience to. There were no repeat performances, nothing more was ever mentioned of *The Unspeakable Mysteries*, and nine months later Anna Leibowitz walked into the ocean, immersing herself in eternal silence.

IRVING, WHEN WE finally met two years later at a symphony

benefit, seemed to bear no grudge against me. My review of his wife's concert was never mentioned. In fact, it was Irving who encouraged me on that very evening to take up orchestral farming. "Follow your heart's desire," Irving told me. "Cultivate your appetites." He promised seeds to get me started and told me of other farmers who would be glad to help. The next spring I moved to a ten-acre estate, suitable for planting, and it's been a successful enterprise ever since.

Until, that is, the trouble with my cellos.

IT'S A TRADITION. Every harvest season I have students from the university come help take in my crop. Afterwards I prepare a huge feast at which we gorge ourselves on sonance and timbre, playing upon the cornucopia of my new harvest. Irving—who'd been to my home only one time before, the day he brought my first seeds – well, Irving showed up unexpectedly for my fall harvest. I was delighted to have him there, especially to show him first-hand the rotted, gnarled, a-tonal fruition of his ungodly seeds.

"Well, there they are," I said, acerbically, pointing to the menacing crop. The cellos were as black as pitch, their necks as thin as corn stalks, their distended bellies raw and bristled, and their strings sharp as thorns. He said not a word, but kept his eyes fixed upon them.

It was then that one of my students, Chloe, the untalented daughter of the dean, entered the cello patch. My other students had been diligently gathering up the violins and violas. Cords of brass horns were stacked neatly inside the storage shed. Woodwinds were being hosed off at the side of the house beneath the piano trellis. It was getting dark – rain clouds threatening a storm – and I urged them to hurry and to leave the cellos behind.

I was about to walk over, remind Chloe of this, when

Irving grabbed my sleeve, pulling me back. Chloe, with a bow plucked from its vine, began drawing forth a long, vociferous moan from one of the deformed cellos.

The other students dropped what they were doing to see the source of these strange emanations. An untended garden hose flooded the lawn. Two flashlights turned upon her lone figure, squatting in the garden, legs astride the black-shelled cello. Chloe was absorbed in her playing, head arched back revealing a long neck like a chalk column. The strings seemed to sob and shiver, gradually building into a series of rising intervals of whole tones followed by semitones. Then came an earthly rumble that, for a moment, seemed an extension of her playing, but gradually became discernible as an approaching storm.

Winds picked up as her playing took on more frantic gestures. Chloe lowered her head revealing features now dark and narrow, eyes reflecting light the way transfixed nocturnal animals often do. These were the features of Anna Leibowitz that had stayed in my mind for so many years. And this, yes, this was the same intense cacophony which Anna Leibowitz had created many years before. The sky cracked open with brilliant exclamations of light and thunder. Rain hailed down. Students hurried to gather the last of the instruments, bringing them indoors. And Leibowitz, the old man, nearly deaf, with withered hands, dropped to his knees. And from his eye poured bitter tears of adoration.

X-24

Naomi Alderman

The Matchmaker of Hendon

My mother was a spinner of tales both tall and long. There was the story of the Tailor's Tallit, which proves that a garment can be too much admired, the legend of the Bencher of Babylon, whose words may be read, but never spoken, and the tale of the Herring Bride and what became of her one true love. But these stories were not her best. She told her best story only twice: once to me, when I was a child and once to my own children, six months before she died. It was the tale of the Matchmaker of Hendon, the finest matchmaker in the world.

Matchmakers, my mother told the children, used to be more plentiful than they are now. It was, she sighed, a time when concern for one's place in heaven was greater than today. For do we not learn that one who makes three successful matches guarantees thereby her seat in the world to come? Yes, there were matchmakers for the religious and the not-so-religious, for the Zionist and the Chareidi, for the Liberal, the Progressive, the Satmar and the Gerer. Not like today. In those days, to be the best matchmaker in the world, you really had to be something. You'd think, then, that the Matchmaker of Hendon was maybe raised and schooled in the art? That she trained with the great matchmakers of Paris, Jerusalem and New York? Not so. In fact, for many years she taught the piano to children.

"Like Zeida?" my children interrupted.

"Yes," replied my mother, "like your grandfather, the Matchmaker of Hendon was a piano teacher. Now, do you want to tell the story or shall I?"

Day by day, young people passed through the Matchmaker's home, sullen or studious, reluctant or eager. She saw that her role was not simply to teach these youths to strike the keys, but also to find the music which was most suited to them. And as her pupils grew to adulthood, she began to see patterns not only within each student but also between them. She made her first match between two of her students, then between a student and a friend's child. As time went on, she began to discern suitable matches between people she had merely glanced, or spoken with for a few moments. It became obvious that she possessed a gift.

The Matchmaker of Hendon, we may note in passing, was herself unmarried. She came to feel that this gave her an 'ear' for matchmaking, just as one can more truly appreciate music if one is not humming a contrary tune. And so, over time, she came to be known as a talented matchmaker.

***

MY MOTHER PAUSED.

"So far," she said, "so what?"

My children blinked.

"Yes," she said, "so what? So she'd made a few matches. No big deal." She waved her hand airily. "Who hasn't made a few matches? That just made her a matchmaker. Not the finest in the world. No, it took something else to win her that title. But eh, I don't know if you're really interested in this story. Maybe you're tired?"

Once the clamour died down, my mother continued.

The Matchmaker of Hendon's most celebrated case concerned the son of a certain Rabbi. This young man was bright, pleasant, learned in Torah, gentle of heart and neatly-trimmed of beard: all that a bride could wish. But he was marred by a peculiar affliction. He perspired. All men perspire, of course, but this youth was exceptional. In general not inclined to sweat, when he became interested by a young woman moisture poured from him, and with it a pungent and unappealing smell. The more attracted he was, the more foul the scent. The odour, which was equally uncontrollable by lotion, cream or pill, was enough to deter any woman. In desperation, he sought out Matchmaker of Hendon and pleaded for her aid. After he left her, she sat, as was her habit, in a chair overlooking the window, stirring her tea very slowly, sipping with very small sips, and thinking very deeply indeed. At last, decisive, she drank the tea to its dregs, stood up and made a single telephone call.

Three months later, the malodorous young man was married. At the wedding, the guests naturally declared that the groom was wise and learned, and the bride beautiful and virtuous but, in truth, only the virtue and wisdom of the Matchmaker were fully discussed. The bride was attractive, kind and gentle, marred by only one tiny flaw. As a child, she had fallen from a swing onto her nose. Its appearance was not damaged, but the blow had deprived her forever of a sense of smell. All odours were as one to her, neither pleasing nor displeasing. When, ten months later, the couple gave birth to a baby girl, she was of course, named for the Matchmaker.

After this, the Matchmaker of Hendon had no need to seek work. From Argentina and Brazil, Australia and South Africa, Israel, France, India, Portugal, Russia and Abyssinia, parents and children sought her aid. And the wider her circle of clients, the more perfect her matches became, each one more inspired than the last, until the people of Hendon began to declare that she had been given a part of the matchmaking skill which the Holy One Blessed Be He reserves for Himself.

***

"Now," MY MOTHER said, lowering her brows and glaring darkly, "perhaps the Matchmaker became too proud and needed to be taught a lesson. Or perhaps someone else was jealous, and cast the Ayin Hara on her. The Evil Eye is real, you know, so you must always wear your red hendels, no matter what modern nonsense your mother tells you." The children held up their left wrists, displaying the red threads tied around them. My mother nodded, satisfied. "Very good. The Matchmaker of Hendon wasn't so clever, which might explain what happened next."

Now the Matchmaker of Hendon's name had become an incantation in the minds of the people. No one ever came to her single and left without their perfect mate. No one. It came to be believed that she could not fail. But when such a spell is woven, it only takes one failure for the entire vision to be destroyed. And so, upon a day, a new client came to call.

This young man had been one of the Matchmaker's piano pupils. In fact, he brought several pieces of his own to play for her. As he began, the Matchmaker of Hendon reflected on how charming he was, his playing still shy, though much improved, his broad shoulders slightly hunched with nervousness. Yes, she thought, she would have no difficulty finding a suitable girl. She was touched by his pieces, by their simplicity, humour and gentle emotion. When he had finished playing, she told him so. Their discussion lasted several hours.

The Matchmaker of Hendon was a woman of regular and methodical habits. She worked for six days, and on the seventh she rested. From 8am to 4pm, with half an hour for lunch, she met clients and arranged matches. At 4pm, she took a walk around Hendon, to exercise her limbs, buy her groceries and, perhaps, encounter some grateful parent along the way (for modesty was not one of her primary virtues and she enjoyed receiving praise for her work). At 5pm she drank tea, very slowly, and considered the clients she had met that day. From 6 to 7 was her dinner hour. At 7pm she spread her accounts wide, and sent out her invoices. And from 8.30 to 10pm she received telephone calls informing her of the success of the meetings she had arranged. Her life went forward as rhythmically as the sweeping arm of the metronome. It was some surprise to her therefore to find, when the young man left, that her hour for walking in Hendon had already passed, as had her hour for tea. But, she reflected, if she could not interrupt her routine for an old friend, when could she?

The following day, she set to work on behalf of the young man. She selected a girl. She arranged a meeting. The meeting took place a few days later. The girl telephoned that evening: she had been enchanted, could scarcely wait for the second meeting, thought he might be *the one*. The young man telephoned shortly afterward. He inquired after the Matchmaker's health, and asked whether she might be interested in looking over some new piano books. Yes yes, but the girl, what about the girl? Oh the girl had been fine enough, but not for him.

The Matchmaker frowned as she replaced the receiver. It had been over three months since she had had to arrange a *second* match. Her first choices were usually faultless. But no matter, she would make another attempt. That evening, as she ate her customary slice of plava cake, she found that she was drumming her fingers on the tabletop and thought that, in their rhythm, she heard the faintest sound of laughter.

The second girl would not do either. Nor would the third. Nor the fourth. It was not that they did not like him. But he appeared to be seeking something which none of them possessed. The young man became a regular visitor in the Matchmaker's house. Together they agonised over possible choices. They played the piano while debating the qualities of a certain girl from Bratislava or another from Sao Paulo. They swapped sheet music while passing suggestions back and forth of experts they might consult. They agreed, each time, that the next choice would be perfect. But each time it was the same: the young piano player would not settle on a match.

He became notorious in Hendon. Other young people came to the Matchmaker's door, found their allotted partner, and departed content. This boy, the people said, would reach 120 before he was satisfied with a girl. Perhaps, they murmured, all was not well with him. Perhaps his desires were not as the desires of other men. Or maybe the Matchmaker of Hendon had lost her gift. One or two young people began to seek advice from other matchmakers. One or two became six or seven, then fifteen or twenty and at last the rumours found their way to the Matchmaker's ears.

She was shocked. This would not do, she thought. It was not orderly. Her life, which had proceeded as smoothly as a sonata, as regularly as a rondo, for so many years, had become suddenly discordant, filled with faulty fingering. She decided challenge the young man regarding his behaviour. She telephoned him that evening, at the appropriate hour.

But she found the conversation rather difficult to begin; they had so many other things to discuss. At last, she blurted:

"Are you experiencing any emotional difficulties?"

The line was silent. The Matchmaker could hear the young piano player breathing, softly.

"Not as far as I'm aware," he replied.

"Then," she said, banging her hand on the table, "why have you not yet chosen a girl? I have found you ten and ten times ten! Are you sure you are quite well?"

The line became silent again, the young man's breathing slow and steady. The Matchmaker looked around her quiet, tidy home, taking in the lace tablecloth and the polished brass bell on her mantelshelf. She felt suddenly afraid of what she had done.

"Perhaps," he said, "I love someone already."

The Matchmaker thought for a moment that her telephone was faulty. There seemed to be a ringing on the line, or in her ear. She shook the handset and said:

"Hello? Hello?"

"I'm here," the young man said. "But I must go now. I'll see you tomorrow. For tea."

The next morning, the Matchmaker awoke angry. When she opened the curtains, she tugged too hard, and the pole fell to the ground. When she telephoned, she dialled seven wrong numbers in succession. In frustration, she picked at the beads on the cuff of her blouse, pulling off first one, then another, until a small shining heap was piled on the table and she realised the she had ruined the garment. She let out a cry. It was, she thought, too much. Imagine visiting a matchmaker when he was already in love! It was an insult to her profession, an insult to the girls she had found for him. Why, it was no wonder she was angry!

When she returned from her Hendon walk that

afternoon, her spirits were not improved. The exercise had only increased her annoyance so that, when she approached her home and heard the unmistakeable notes of piano-playing falling from the open window, her anger ignited into fury. Even if she did leave her door open, how dare he enter her home? Play her piano? Pretend to be something he was not? She burst into her living room and began to shout. The music was stronger. The young man's head was bowed over the piano; he simply continued to play. She saw that the piece was written in his own hand, and its notes were more than words. And as he played, she understood. And when his playing was done the room hummed, resonating where there had once been stillness.

"Whom do you love?" she asked, though she already knew.

The young man turned his head to her. And upon his face was a smile, and in his smile she read the answer to her question. And she knew that her answer was the same as his. And she began to weep.

"Children," my mother said, "they loved each other. What joy! But what a catastrophe! Whoever heard of a matchmaker falling in love with her client? The Matchmaker of Hendon was past her middle years, but the young piano player was just a boy of twenty-two. They despaired as soon as they understood the truth, for his parents would never accept it. And without help from his parents, how were they to live? The people of Hendon would not trust a matchmaker who had married her young client. The pair tasted sweetness and bitterness in the same bite."

My mother paused. The children grew impatient.

"What happened then, Booba? What happened then?"

My mother looked at the faces of the children. Her eyes were tender, as soft as water. She opened her mouth to speak and closed it again.

"What happened then, Booba?"

My mother smiled a strange and unexpected smile. She spoke quickly, as though trying to utter the words before she heard them.

"They were married, of course. They found that all their friends and family were far more forgiving than they'd expected. In fact, the Matchmaker became even busier than before, because now, of course, she was happily married herself. Yes, they were married for years and years and had children and grandchildren. The grandchildren were just like you except not *quite* so beautiful or so clever. Now, who wants rogelach?"

The children yelled and raised a forest of hands.

I stood in silence. I had not remembered the tale ending so abruptly.

***

LATER, AFTER THE children were in bed, my mother and I drank tea together.

"Mummy," I said, "how does the story really end?"

"What? What story?"

"The story you told the children, the Matchmaker of Hendon."

My mother frowned.

"I told you how it ended. They got married and lived happily ever after. Don't you know a good ending when you hear it?"

She took another sip of tea.

"But when you told it to me years ago, didn't it have a different ending?"

My mother placed her cup upon its saucer.

"And what do you think that was?"

"I don't know. Something different. More sad. More true."

"Well." She rubbed her brow. "I'm very tired boobelah. Another time, maybe?"

I took her hand and pressed it, inexplicably determined to hear the end.

"No," I said, "tonight. Tell me tonight. Please."

She made me wait until she was in bed, her lamp lit, pillows around her.

"So, my child, the Matchmaker of Hendon was in a terrible position. What could she do? If they married her career would be over, and he was in no position to support her. If she failed to find him a match, her reputation would be ruined. There was only one solution."

"What did they do?"

"What do you think?"

I shook my head.

"They talked through the night, but all their plots and plans led back to one solution. She proposed it, in fact. He refused for seven days. Each time they spoke, she insisted it was the only course. Each time, he refused. But on the seventh day, he saw that she'd become weak with sadness and, in despair, agreed to her proposal."

"But what did they do?"

"She found him a girl, of course. What else could they do? If they married, how would they live? He protested; he was younger and more foolish. He said they would find a way to be together, that love would find a way. She smiled and touched his cheek, but she knew in her heart that *love* does not make a good match. A good match needs a good matchmaker.

"So she chose a girl for him. A perfectly acceptable, pleasant young woman. And for love of the Matchmaker, he married this other girl, although until the night before his wedding he begged her to reconsider. The guests at the wedding repeated stories of the Matchmaker's prowess, and her livelihood was saved. But you know," my mother leaned up on her elbows, "they said that after that she lost her skill, little by little. She'd lost a sense for it, you see. Or maybe she'd betrayed whatever power it was that gave her the gift. Her matches started to fail. She would introduce dozens of couples, with no success. One or two of the matched she made ended in," my mother lowered her voice, "divorce. Her reputation went, for all they'd tried to save it. She died broken-hearted and empty-pursed. But, though her gift failed at the end, she had made her three matches, and three times thrice three and more." My mother laughed, a short, rattling bark. "That woman had enough merit to get all of us through the gates and into the world to come."

"And the young piano player and his wife?"

"It took the wife," my mother's mouth worked, "it took her years to understand where her husband's affections lay. And when she did, what could she do?" My mother sighed. "She had her life. She simply carried on.

"The young piano player became a piano teacher, like his beloved. He and his wife had a daughter and they lived," my mother closed her eyes for a long moment. "They lived with a certain measure of happiness. No one can say that they did not. And the piano player who became a piano teacher grew to be an old man, and passed to his reward. But I think," my mother placed her hand on mine, the skin paper-thin and dusted with liver spots. She squeezed my hand. "I think he always loved her. Until the day he died. And I never told him that I knew. No, I never told him."

She turned her head toward the pillow. Within a few seconds she was asleep.

CLAIRE SHARLAND

Eel Stew

THE WIND STAMPEDED across the fen, pushing her over the road. The army surplus overcoat she had inherited from mother flapped open at the front like a tent, telltale clumps of broken thread marking the place where two buttons were missing. Mother would be angry and call her slattern.

Though if she noticed, she had said nothing yet. Perhaps in death her conscience had finally found her out.

- Get a move on dear. And do your coat up.

- Just having a breather.

- You've been dilly-dallying all morning. He'll be gone if you don't hurry up.

- I had to wait for the storm to pass.

Mother snorted. She never would have waited; they both

knew that. She would have set off in gum boots, a plastic bag tied over her head and another stuffed into her pocket in which to carry back the bounty. Liza would be left watching the small bent figure hastening towards the river from the window of their flat above, rain streaming down the other side of the glass to which she pressed her hand.

The path to the riverbank was slippery with mud, though the wind dropped once they were off the road. Much of the land to her left was submerged, three broken-backed trees like signposts in the water. She could feel the presence of the converted old mill, home for so long, brooding behind her. Liza kept her weight forward on the balls of her feet to prevent her heels from sinking into the ground. Suede ankle boots may not be the best footwear for the conditions, but she would never be able to bring herself to wear mother's wellies, still standing caked with dried mud on newspaper in the hallway, a man's sock tucked in and turned over the top of each. Though she did rather regret the broderie-anglaise petticoat; the lace had become splashed with mud, and she looked like a harlot.

Mother found that idea very amusing.

- *Well, if you will insist on getting up theatrical,* she said, once she had stopped laughing. - *What's he supposed to think!*

Liza ignored her. Mother had always been so dour, with long black skirts and grey hair scraped into a bun. And he could think what he liked. If she hadn't missed him. She hoped she hadn't missed him.

He looked down at his hands busy with rope as her eyes met his in the distance. He had been watching her then. Head down, she made her way along the river bank. Why did he let her keep on coming? The dealer from London paid him much more than she could. He must still be as much in mother's thrall as she was. She pictured him standing in his socks in the confines of their apartment, staring off into a dusty corner whilst mother knelt before him with a mouth full of pins, adjusting the leg of his latest suit. His was a hard life, mother said. Once an eel fisherman could make a handsome living, but stocks were dwindling, and things changed. Mother kept a hip flask in her coat pocket to offer him, which he would lift in a silent toast to her before he drank.

He nodded as Liza slowed to a halt before him.

"Was beginning to think you weren't going to make it today."

"I was waiting for the rain to stop."

"Yeah. These September storms."

He bent to his net, anchoring it to a peg in the ground. The river pulled past them, swollen and urgent with all the recent rain. He had chewed his fingernails down to the quick. 'All those hours on the river bank alone,' mother whispered. Liza closed her eyes, the lids suddenly heavy. When she opened them, he was studying her keenly, lines etched delicate and precise at the corner of his green eyes.

"Are you o.k.?"

"Yes. Thanks."

She forced a smile. He turned to untie the neck of the keep net on the ground beside him. The eels inside were turbulent, excited by the smell of the water so close. The second run of silvers. The females would have left before the harvest. Those that had escaped the nets would be half-way round the world. He pulled one out, grasping it behind the head. Their small triangular teeth were sharp with a powerful bite, and this eel knew nothing but its desperation for the saltiness of the Sargasso Sea singing along its skin. The long muscular body, dark and gleaming along the back, thrashed against him, and he seized it with his other hand before it could whip itself around his arm in a grip that would be difficult to loose. It twisted in mid-air, one pale-blue disc of an eye fixing on Liza. She shuddered. The only salt it would savour now would be seasoning for the pot.

"Where's your bag?"

His voice strained. She pulled the string bag quickly from her pocket. Once inside, the eel became subdued, glowering with resentment at this new and more specialized confinement, glossy skin bulging against the twine. She handed him a ten pound note, and he dug in his pocket for change. His jeans were worn to a pale blue, darker across the thighs where soaked. Her eye travelled stealthily along the inside seam, searching for the shape of him underneath.

- *So which way does sir wear his trousers!*

Mother's bellow made her jump, and Liza looked up panicked that he had heard it too. But he continued counting money in the palm of his hand. He held out a column of coins between finger and thumb.

"Sorry about the change."

She reached out to take it, but not quite far enough, and the money fell, scattering in the grass. He squatted down to help her retrieve it, their heads so close she dared not breathe.

- *Slut.*

Not now mother, please.

- *Do you think I don't know, what it is you want? Well, go on. Have him. Right here, with you knickers round your ankles and your legs flailing in the mud. After all, some things can't wait, can they dear? And let's face it, you've waited long enough. So what's stopping you? Go on then. Don't hold back on my account!*

Hand over mouth to stop the whimpering that escaped her, Liza fled. He called something after her, but his words were indistinct, drowned out by her mother's that were so much closer.

- *Sorry love. But you wouldn't want to go making a fool of yourself, now would you?*

The bag with the eel slapped against her leg as she struggled back towards the road. Her hair got into her eyes so she couldn't see where she was going, and she skidded, the eel almost slithering off into the ditch. As she fought to get it back into the bag, she found herself struggling not to cry.

- *What a poor feeble thing you are. Whatever do you think he might   see in you?*

- *You're only saying that because you want him to yourself. You're jealous, because you're dead, and I can do what I want!*

Everything was abruptly still. Only a thrush, perched on the barbed wire in the hedgerow dared move, cocking its head on one side to peer at her. 'You've done it now,' it seemed to say. 'She'll never speak to you again.' And flew off over her head. On the other side of the fence, the sun began to roll out from behind the cloud.

DAMP FOOTPRINTS LED across the black and white tiles to where she sat with her back against the fridge, ruined boots in the hallway next to mother's. Coming up the stairs to their front door, she had imagined that mother would be waiting to welcome her home; that her outburst would be forgiven. But the flat was empty. In the sink, the eel beat a tattoo against the metal sides.

She drew her cardigan about her. Despite the bright patch of sky at the window, the kitchen was in twilight. The eel became still, resigned to its ritual part in the proceedings. Maybe she should begin peeling the potatoes. If she started preparations mother would have to speak to her, to give instructions as she always had. It was mother's recipe after all. Mince the garlic, slice the shallots, chop the carrots, parsley, grate the zest of lemon and the nutmeg, get the butter and rashers of bacon from the fridge, put the water on to boil. Then everything would be ready. She hated what came next. The gallon saucepan loomed on the opposite wall, the pliers for skinning on the next hook. Mother knew that she wouldn't be able to go through with it without her. Perhaps the waiting was a test.

Once she had filled the saucepan from the tap and put it on the ring, she took the flask of red wine that mother had brewed just months before from the cupboard under the sink and poured herself a drink. To keep her company. Surely mother would allow that. She stood and watched the eel shifting in the sink as she drank. It was the head, blunt-nosed yet domed at the temple like an egg, that gave them such a strange, primitive appearance. She ran some water so he could splash about, and carried the wine into the living room.

The old singer was still threaded. She sat at the stool, and turned the wheel. The whir of machinery was startling in the quiet. Her long hair had got caught under the foot once, the treadle running away with her so she was dragged towards the plunging needle, until her neck was cricked and her cheek flat against the metal plate. Mother had said that it was the best line of stitching that she had ever done, and that it would be a shame to unpick it. Now she could get her own machine, one that responded to her alone. No longer was she anybody's apprentice. She struck hard at the metronome on the cabinet next to her with the side of her hand. It swung into motion; back, forth, clack, clack; with the rhythm that mother had claimed helped her concentrate when sewing. The sound seemed to echo from another lifetime.

Kneeling down on the rug alongside, she pulled mother's workbox from its place against the wall. The lacquered surface reflected her face like a mirror, a sudden and intimate glimpse of herself that made her flinch.

It was hard to believe that such an inscrutable exterior concealed the concertina of compartments she knew so well, containing things that she had been allowed to handle, to remove and replace as they were needed. Top left – tailor's chalk, glass-headed pins of multi colours stabbed into the heart-shaped pin cushion she had made as a child; top right – needles – sharps, chenille and glovers for leather work, silver thimble, the blue-handled awl for button holes in the tier below, seam ripper, stitch ripper, a card of leather buttons; and in the largest chamber at the bottom, pinking shears and bent handled fabric scissors, the orange handles vying with the crimson of the lining. Half expecting the release of some occult and violent power, she opened out the box. Nothing happened. Only a rattling sound as she kicked it away from her across the floor. Things wouldn't be so well-ordered inside now. She drained her glass and refilled it. The sharp edges of the room were beginning to dissolve.

Glass in hand, she stood up and pulled out the drawers of the cabinet, emptying elastic, belt-buckles, hook and eyes, press studs, zips and reels of thread out onto the floor. She ripped up old patterns, and chucked rolls of pin stripe, worsted, gabardine and calico, the fabric unravelling in a gracious arc as it traversed the room. Stumbling, she knocked over the dressmaker's mannequin, and cheered as she watched it fall.

Stepping over the prone figure into the middle of the room, she discovered she could dance to the rhythm of the metronome; clack clack; pivoting on one leg until she was whirling about the room like a dervish. Her hair streamed about her head, arms spiralling high; clack clack; and she opened her mouth to holler. Then there was mother, at last, watching her from the edge of the circle, and there she was again, and again; and she was laughing too, for joy; clack clack. And there was he, clapping her round. She had conjured them up; clap clap. He urged her on with his eyes that alighted on her every time she passed, on her breast, her thigh, her hair.

She collapsed into a chair. He and mother were still circling about each other, from the floor to the ceiling in giddy reels. She giggled.

"Stop it. Stay still. I can't see you."

Then there were just their faces, swimming before her. They were smiling, but then she shut her eyes, just for a second, and when she opened them they were gone.

She stood up so suddenly the chair fell behind her. Running into the kitchen, she took the pan of boiling water from the stove, and emptied it into the sink. The eel flailed helplessly. From the armchair in the other room, hugging her knees and rocking gently to and fro, she waited for the thrashing to stop, watching the sun sink down below the horizon like a blazing ship.

WITH THE POT of stew chuckling on the stove, she sat with mother's coat across her knees, the heavy wool tickling her legs through the stuff of her tights, sewing on the missing buttons. Dusk was deepening across the fen. Her head singing a little, she took a sip of water from the glass beside her chair.

It was restful to be curled up in the velvet interior of the armchair. This was the hour she had always looked to. With the eel's torment over, the skinning and chopping done, the kitchen windows steaming up and darkness falling outside, she would sit where she was now and mother would brush her hair. She would pull at first, but the zeal she expended in killing changed her, gracing her with a new benevolence. Eyes shining and dewy wet, she would fall into a strong but gentle rhythm, and Liza would be lulled by the lilt of her head back at every stroke. It was now that mother told her about eels, in loving tones so low that sometimes the words were lost. Though it didn't matter. Liza had heard the stories so often they were part of her own. That the dried skin of an eel, ground to a powder in a pestle and mortar and mixed with wine, was an aphrodisiac that cured many other ills besides. How the ancients had believed the species generated from the mud in which they live, and how they were once the food of kings. How they live wild and singular, roaming unseen through the water for up to a decade, knowing nothing of their loneliness. Until one day a craving awakes, and they eat and eat to appease it, until their stomachs wither with their appetite and they never eat again. And they wait, skulking on the beds of rivers, ponds and dykes. Then, always on a dark September night, the call comes. Three thousand miles across the ocean. Some thought, mother said, that they navigate their way to the Sargasso Sea by the stars. There a whole company gathers, under the shadow of the weed floating on the surface. The females hang ripe in the water; the male swims between, searching. She waits, with the patience of a lifetime. And then he finds her. As the slither of new matter ascends the shaft of sunlight that penetrates from the world above, the parents spiral downwards through the darkness, their bodies landing on the seabed with a silent crash. Particles rise and settle. Then, stillness.

WITH A FULL moon, there would be no eels travelling tonight. Through the window there was the glint of a star, then another, then too many to count underpinning the vast architecture of the night sky. She was sorry that the eel's sacrifice had been for nothing.

IT WAS GETTING too dark to sew. She reached up to turn on the lamp, and found herself gazing at her reflection in the window.

Mother had been old as long as she could remember. But in the days before she died, she became soft, without definition or resolve, and shuffled from room to room as if in a dream. When Liza placed a hand gently on her shoulder, she would pat it, once, twice, before pushing it away.

At table, she ate staring off into infinity, lifting her food slowly to her mouth like a child, ill-fitting teeth hitting the metal of the spoon with a clunk that made Liza want to smack it from her hand. So when mother's spoon did clatter to her bowl, Liza thought she must have struck her after all; mother was so white and gasping. There was a noise in her throat as if something was trying to escape, and she toppled to the floor with her chair, Liza falling to her knees beside her. She remembered noticing how waxy mother's scalp was, a bloodless scratch from the comb at the parting, and there being a high pitched whine in her ears. Then there was quiet, as if the room had been full of din and noise and people, and then suddenly everyone had left.

SHE SNIPPED THROUGH the thread, and tugged at the heavy button to make sure it was secure. Mother would be pleased. Though it was too late for that now. She felt suddenly empty, her stomach sucking to her backbone for warmth. Stiff from having sat still for so long, she uncurled her legs from under her, and went into the kitchen.

The pan was decorated with a trail of white ferment down the side where it had boiled over. She took the silver tureen from the cupboard, and heaped it full before carrying it through into the other room, placing it in front of the single place laid at the head of the table. She sat down and lifted the lid. Steam billowed like a genie. Ravenous now, she ladled stew into her bowl, careless to spillage on the tablecloth. She took a morsel of potato and some liquor from her spoon. It scalded the roof of her mouth. The skin would come away in tatters later, but for now she gulped down food as fast as she could. The red wine she had added to the sauce was good, cutting through the rich sweetness of the eel. Devouring mouthful after mouthful, bowlful after bowlful, she gorged herself. Her eyes and nose were streaming it was so hot, so she used her serviette to wipe away the snot and tears whilst eating. She couldn't stop. If mother had been there she would have been ashamed. As it was, the glimpses of life that surfaced in her mind could have belonged to someone else; mother raising her hip flask with the river behind; the coveted glimpse of the shape of his prick in his jeans; the hunch of mother's shoulders as she lay lifeless on the floor.

Something lurched within her. Her first thought was that the eel had reformed and was rising in her gullet, so she was relieved when it was pieces of fish, potato, carrot that rose with a rush of wine into the toilet bowl, her body relinquishing them with such ease and abundance it was almost sensual. But when her stomach was empty, it kept on wringing her so she retched, though there was nothing left to come up but bile. Her body finally purged, she lay on the bathroom floor, the tiles cool against her cheek. She closed her eyes, and imagined herself reeling out across the sky and between the stars, the river far below.

THERE WAS NO-ONE ahead of her at the bus stop. She was in plenty of time. The sunlight was warm and scintillating, the hedgerow abundant with berries; scarlet, and wanton inky black. Her step rang out even and sure in the morning so full of promise, her small unsupported breasts jolting beneath the material of her blouse at every strike of a heel on the road. After she had bought her new sewing machine, she would treat herself to lunch, with an ice-cream sundae.

"Liza."

She had not heard her name uttered since before mother died. She stopped, turning slowly.

His boots and jeans were muddy from the river bank. He shrugged the weight of a keep net across his shoulder, the hoops of a fyke net over the other. She waited for him to speak.

"You forgot your change. You know, the other day."

So that was all it was. Well, he could keep it. She didn't want to be reminded what a fool she must have seemed, running off like that. But he was searching his pockets with his free hand.

" I don't have it on me now, but I'll give it to you next time."

She nodded, thinking that there wouldn't be a next time, that she had done with eels, and with him.

"Liza. Liza are you alright? It must be hard, you know, with your mother…"

His voice tailed off. How readily he spoke her name suddenly. She tried to remember his. She must know it. Simon. That was it. Of course. Simon.

She heard a movement; the scrape of a boot along the surface of the road. He had taken a step towards her, and she realised she had said his name aloud. The shape of it lingered in her mouth. Then she heard the drone of the bus on the top road, and ran for it as fast as she could.

HER SEWING MACHINE gleamed newly minted on the table before her. She had dragged mother's singer into the corner, where it had become just another piece of furniture, a handy surface on which to put things. She would put an advert in the gazette – *'Bespoke tailoring for men and women.'* She would make dresses from silks of glowing jewel-like colours, slinky skirts of crepe, blouses, dress shirts, waistcoats, collars and suits, for evening and everyday wear.

The doorbell made her jump. Probably a neighbour,

come to complain about the noise of things being dragged over the floor. If she didn't answer they would go away. It came again, a short, faltering burst. They were losing faith, and would leave without her ever knowing who it was. She bolted for the door.

He was at the top of the stairs as she opened it, one foot ready to descend the first step. He was carrying something, which as he came forward onto the landing she saw was an eel, smoked, its desiccated head protruding from the newspaper it was wrapped in. He hesitated, seeming to be unsure suddenly why he had come. Then he pointed to the faded card by the doorbell and shrugged, lifting his arms from his sides and grinning as if admitting to something foolish.

"I need a new suit."

She stood staring at the paraphernalia inside the cabinet. The tape measure and notebook she needed were on the top shelve, in easy reach. He stood behind her in the middle of the room, hands listless at his sides now the eel had been given up and was on the marble top in the kitchen. He had removed his jumper, almost taking the t-shirt underneath with it, and arranged his boots with great care at the edge of the rug, moving them minutely until they were side by side, exactly as he wanted. He must be wondering why she took so long.

She advanced towards him. Using her thigh to rest on, she recorded his measurements in the notebook, pressing hard into the paper with her pencil. *Half back: 9.2 inches.* She had never been this close to him. She concentrated on dissecting him into parts. *Depth from neck to mid-point between shoulder blades: 10.6 inches.* She could smell him, the seaside tang of sweat with the cleanliness of soap. *Trouser waist: 39 inches.* He lifted his arms so she could pass the tape measure around his chest. As she leant in towards him, her breasts brushed his back.

Exhilaration began to rise as she moved around him. Mother might be dead, but she was here, with him. She had weight, significance. Efficiency.

"Can you bend your arm please?"

Obediently, he gave himself up as she turned him this way and that, though his face was tense as he stared past her into the corner of the room. *Sleeve length, for a two piece: 33.5 inches.* Perhaps her fingers lingered as she took the tape from his wrist. He shifted uneasily, his breath quickening. *Close wrist measurement: 7.4.*

She knelt beside him on the rug. His socks, thick grey wool flecked with brown, made his feet look like the paws of an animal she would like to pet.

He leapt away so suddenly she fell backwards onto the floor.

"I'm sorry. I didn't think. It was a stupid idea. I don't need a suit."

He looked about wildly for his jacket. Finding it flung over the back of the armchair, he stood clutching it in front of him.

"I just needed to know you were alright. You seemed so upset the other day. Your mum would want someone to look out for you."

She grinned. She couldn't help it. He looked so woebegone, and she guessed what he took such care to keep hidden beneath his jacket. He reddened under her scrutiny, and made a move towards his boots, just a few feet from where she sat.

But she got there first, scuttling in a rush so that the rug skidded on the floorboards and they collided. She felt the impact of his knee against her cheek, but laughed out loud. She still had his boots.

"Please, Liza."

He held out his hand as if annoyed, though he smiled, despite himself.

She threw the heavy boots one to either side of her; clunk, clunk; and reached up to pull his jacket, still held in front of him as a shield, from his grasp.

As he realised what she intended, a look of disbelief, almost panic, crossed his face. Though he offered no resistance as she undid first his belt, then his flies, and took him in her mouth.

PETER HOBBS

Waterproof

WE'RE IN THE pub waiting for Harry. Nestor is making his usual complaints about exhaustion in a voice loud enough that we're getting strange looks from the drinkers. Not disapproving looks, just strange ones. I can't breathe for laughing. Shafique and Jay Jay are nodding politely and sipping their cokes even though I know they're finding it just as funny as I am. It's just that they feel they're supposed to disapprove of this kind of thing, so they hide it. Nestor pauses to take a huge gulp of his own coke and draw breath. I choke on a mouthful of lager and spew it all over my lap. It's lucky I'm still wearing my waterproofs.

"It's the minerals," Nestor is saying. "I think I have malnutrition."

He's looking paler, it's true.

The weird thing is that Nestor works the hardest of us all and he doesn't wash a single car. He's a legend in the forecourt.

"Today's the day," he says every morning. "Today I'm going to wash more cars than all of you motherfuckers put together."

And then even as we're busy filling the buckets – before we've even begun our daily game of *Wash!*, which we always lose anyway because we're always a man short – the first car pulls in and gives us the signal and Nestor marches right over. And the woman – it's not always a woman, but the first one is usually a young mother coming in for her daily shop right after the school run – takes one look at him and they both get in the car and drive off. Every day, I swear. An hour or two later she drives back up and drops him off.

"Sheeit," he says. "I thought that was going to be the one."

Ten minutes later and he's gone again – new car, new driver. By then end of the day he's even more exhausted than the rest of us.

"Fuck me," he says wearily, and sometimes you get the feeling he's not even saying this, it's just an echo of what he's been hearing all day. I mean it must be pheromones or something. He's a fucking phenomenon.

"I think you're making it harder than it is," offers Jay Jay. "It's not a difficult job. You just have to wash cars."

"You know I am trying," says Nestor, annoyed. I think it really bothers him.

Basically there's some kind of informal pimping going on here. Nestor is resigned to getting caught and losing his job over it sooner or later, but Harry certainly knows about it already, because he never asks where Nestor is when he comes to check on us, and my feeling is that the supermarket knows about it too – after all, they've blanket CCTV coverage over the car park, and keep a close eye on us to check we don't steal stuff from the cars. They'd notice this kind of thing. But I think too they know that it brings in business – keeps the families shopping here – and they might as well get a piece of the action. They do have a commitment to Customer Service, after all.

And then condom sales are way up, apparently.

Maybe I'm over-stating the case a little. Maybe Nestor has a lot of friends. Maybe these women just need a hand carrying their shopping and I'm only seeing the sex everywhere because I'm not getting any. It's a possibility.

Meantime we pimp ourselves round the car park. Four teams of washers, each with their own bit of concrete turf to operate on. Two guys (just the one on our team, given Nestor's reliable absence) back at the station (a trolley loaded with water containers, buckets and sponges, detergent and windscreen cleaners) waiting for the customer to come to them. Two out on the make. "Car-wash-mate?" "While-you-shop?" There's about a three percent take-up rate, which we work on hard. There are the ones who claim not to have time, who think they can shop faster than we can clean. We offer to do it for free if we're not finished by the time they get back. They pay up.

Quiet times I wander over to talk to Shireen, the only girl on the teams. To be honest, I don't have much of a social life outside of work. Can't really afford it, is the main thing, but I try never to get too far from my mum's place, either. In fact, Shireen is the only girl I actually know to talk to, so perhaps it's not surprising I have a crush on her. It's doing strange things to my head. I'm so insanely fond of her that in the top drawer in my room at my mum's house I keep an umbrella I bought off her once, which I like just because it makes me feel closer to her. I don't even use it – I hate umbrellas. I prefer to get wet.

Shireen gets a lot of stick because she wears marigold rubber gloves to protect her hands, but the truth is that everyone else is just jealous because we didn't think of it first, and we're too proud to copy her, even though our hands are getting slaughtered by the job and at least half of us come down with frostbite in the winter. And she's a fantastic *Wash!* player.

Every day I go over and ask her to come out with me, and every day she says the same thing.

"I don't think my brothers would like that."

At least she's beginning to smile when she says it. Shafique knows one of her brothers, and tells me she's not kidding. There was one time, I'm told, when a customer had been hassling her, and fourteen members from her family fraternity came down to redistribute him.

"How many does she have?" I ask.

"Thirty-two," he says. "Give or take."

"Any sisters?"

"You're not getting this, are you?"

MOST OF THE washers are from Africa. Nigeria, Kenya. The car-park banter passes in a hierarchy of indistinguishable African dialects, but Shafique and Jay Jay do Nestor and me the favour of talking in English. Shafique is appalled I only speak the one language ("How do you communicate with other peoples?"), but there you go.

The employment agency the supermarket uses has hundreds of these guys on the books – newly arrived, poor as fuck. Sometimes the only English they've had time to learn is, "Car wash?" Nestor though is from Guatemala – he and I are freaks of employment. The deal with him is that the only way he could find to get into the country was via Africa, and Immigration took him at his word that he was a

Nigerian with a skin problem and an odd accent. With me it's just the closest work I could find to my mum's place.

In fact I'm the one white guy in the whole car-wash pool. White guys like me are supposed to collect trolleys. I had to beg them to let me work. "Don't you want to go on trolleys?" they asked me. I told them I didn't have a driving license, that I wasn't safe. I have my reasons. The uniform is flexible, for a start. You each get an orange fluorescent waistcoat, a company baseball cap, waterproof trousers. But apart from that you wear what you want.

But anyway, this curious colour divide here: black guys wash cars and white guys collect trolleys. The trolley guys assume they have seniority – after all, they actually work for the store, they get a better basic rate of pay, and they're natives – as far as you can be a native in London. We indulge their innocence. Because what they don't seem to grasp is that we get *tips*. Rounded up pay from mothers too busy dealing with their kids to wait for their change, 50p from a fiver. No one tips them for bringing in the trolleys. And no one is going to pay them on a per-trolley basis. They could push all the trolleys in the world for all the good it'd do them.

Also, that our jobs require an ounce of care and pride and profundity. Listen: dirt is superficial. Our job involves removing the superficial. And that's profound. Of course, as Jay Jay points out, a clean car is a singularly superficial object. So you remove the superficial and you're left with the superficial. How profound is that? I don't hear any of the trolley guys coming up with anything like that. I guess pushing trolleys is functional, doesn't lend itself to philosophy.

To be honest though the washer-pusher rivalry has been on hold a couple of weeks since one of the trolley guys was run over. He was an old guy called Mac, a halfway-house case, a thin man with an alcoholic face, too old for any other work maybe, who found the supermarket to be an equal opportunities employer, at least in the sense that they don't mind geriatric trolley-pushers. Mac was managing a lengthy snake of trolleys, which accumulate in weight when linked together and are, if not exactly difficult to move, at least difficult to stop on a downwards slope.

He was clipped by a black BMW (*Wash!* 12:8:-14), some idiot driving through the car park at rally speeds. The kind who thinks he's a really great driver.

Fucking drivers.

WE JUST HEARD the quick flip-thump, not the familiar crinkle of cars crashing, but something duller, a sound instantly recognisable when you've heard it a few times. It gets you right in the pit of your stomach. Then we looked up to see this long line of trolleys driving themselves perfectly between the rows of cars, headed in the direction of the supermarket, filling the air with the terrible clattering of their wheels.

Worst thing about it was that the Supermarket Manager came on site, had a word in Harry's ear, and we had to give the bloody BMW a complimentary wash. Then we hosed the rest of the gore and bits into a drain. If we actually had a contract, I'm sure as hell that this kind of thing wouldn't be in it.

Harry's our supervisor. He's a fat Hawaiian in a Hawaiian shirt. Likes to stomp around the car park in Bermuda shorts and flip-flops. Only the company cap, fluorescent waistcoat (yellow, for seniority) and clipboard indicate he's doing any kind of a job. Harry's a senior figure in the company. He has contacts, knows people. He oversees four major business forecourts in South London. He doesn't do much when he's round here, though. He keeps an eye on our productivity figures. He gives us marks for our performance. He sacks us if we're caught lazing around. And he sorts out disputes with the customers.

Harry has a bit of a short fuse. Bearing in mind he only oversees work rather than actually doing any, he seems a stressful bloke. The incredible thing about him is that he can't believe he's doing the job he is. He doesn't understand his job, doesn't understand why people want their cars cleaned all the time. "It'll be dirty by tomorrow," he mutters as another recipient of our cleaning expertise leaves the supermarket. He seems to think that these car drivers are, essentially, just wasting our time.

He doesn't even understand why people *have* cars in London. "Insanity," he says as he watches the cars, every one of them entirely empty of passengers, crawl in queues around the forecourt. On the adjacent main road an empty bus hustles uninterrupted down the bus lane.

To be honest I sympathise with him.

And I can see why the clientele gets him down.

For example. There's one guy who drives in with his white Ford Escort (*Wash!* 15:4:22 (for spoiler and wheel arches)) and pulls over, giving us that upwards, beckoning nod of his head which indicates he wants a wash. He's a bulky, gym-built skinhead from one of the nearby estates, and he brings along his girlfriend, a bony adolescent with dyed-blonde hair and a skimpy top. They don't come here to do their grocery shopping. He sits in the driver's seat, door open. She moves over and sits on his lap. They kiss, if you can call it kissing - it's more like mouth-to-mouth sex, lewd and full-on. I've never kissed anyone like that. I'd be too embarrassed, for one thing.

They stay kissing till the car's clean. Loud music on his stereo, needless to say – so loud I can't actually tell what it is, I mean, if it's techno or rock or Bolivian folk music or whatever. It's just too loud. The guy freaks out if he gets splashed with water, though that makes it really hard if you're trying to wash it fast enough to keep your *Wash!* score up, I mean he's got the *door* open.

But here's the thing. He's quite happy for the rest of the team to wash his car, but not me. One day I'd just got started on his windscreen when I noticed that he'd removed his tongue from his girlfriend's throat and was staring at me.

"What the fuck are you doing?" he asks.

I'm confused. "I'm sorry mate, I thought you wanted a wash."

He's confused. "You're a fucking *car-washer?*"

"Well yeah. Sure."

"You can't do this one."

"What's wrong?"

"'cause you'll be fucking looking at my fucking girl that's what the FUCK'S wrong you fucker."

"I won't look. I'll just wash the car. I swear."

"Fuck off. Let one of the you-knows do it."

"What?"

"Oh for fuck's sake. *You* know. One of the you-knows. Africans."

I honestly think he drives in so he can have a black guy wash his car just to show them that he has a car and a girlfriend, as though he's rubbing it in their faces. And he doesn't mind them seeing him making out with his girlfriend because they're black and don't count. It's weird.

Shafique thinks it's hilarious. "Oh, it's so funny. Wait till I tell my mother about this. She's never going to believe me." Shafique is fascinated by him. He washes the guy's car every time he can, and does it with a big smile on his face. Then he wanders over to the public phone, pulls out his phone card, painstakingly keys in a 38-digit number, and chats away to his mum. He has a great laugh. It booms back over towards us, cheers me right up.

RAINY DAYS WE get off. Though rain, of course, is a sliding scale. Mist and drizzle we work. Showers and light rain we standby. Anything heavier than that and we're told to bugger off home. In South London this doesn't exactly constitute a demanding workload, so most people here do other stuff, though I never ask what. Jobs (though there are very few jobs that you can only do on a rainy day apart from selling umbrellas), college. I guess. Personally I usually go home and have some tea with my mum.

Today it's pissing it down. The rain started up early this morning and has settled in since, gradually making itself at home in a familiar and determined way, but we're at work anyway because Harry specifically asked for us.

Of course when we arrived there was no sign of him. And the supermarket is bloody miserable in this weather. We waited at the forecourt for a half hour, sheltering in the trolley section. I was beginning to wish, for more reasons than one, that I was on Shireen's team. Then we left a note on one of the trolleys telling Harry where to find us, and came inside – we'd probably have done that earlier, only the pay's not really good enough that we can just go and sit in the pub all day. Not to mention that there's not much point sitting in the pub all day - none of Shafique, Nestor and Jay Jay actually drinks. Shafique is a Muslim, Jay Jay a Christian, and Nestor is worried about his sperm count. The extent to which their lifestyles subsequently coincide is remarkable.

"After sex, you know, I feel like I have been crucified," Nestor is saying, apparently for Jay Jay's benefit. Jay Jay nods sympathetically.

I like all of these guys, but what I like most about

drinking with them is that even though they're on cokes and I'm on beers they still buy their rounds. I don't think they've worked out that they don't really have to fund my inroads into alcoholism this way. Or maybe they just like to.

"Another round?" I say.

"This one's mine," says Nestor, breaking off from his monologue. Team spirit, after all. And anyway, Nestor does get the largest tips.

When the four of us first started as a team Shafique and Jay Jay were a bit uneasy about each other. There was a bit of religious tension in the air. Shafique goes along to a local mosque, and has been known to disappear around prayer time – there's a mobile mosque which comes around, an old VW camper van (*Wash!* 27:3:3) which pulls up slightly at an angle in the parking space so it's east-facing. Prayer mats in the back. Quite a few of the washers are Muslims and I understand it gets pretty cramped in there. Given the clientele, though, at least it's nice and clean. And Jay Jay belongs to an evangelical church up in Lambeth. One of the things he does on rainy days is street preaching – I bumped into him on Oxford Street in the middle of a thunderstorm one day and he was shouting like crazy. I thought he was sick or on drugs or something and was going over a little nervously to see if I could help him, but he saw me straight off and came over to give me a big hug. Of course he made me listen for a while, so as I could offer him some advice on what really grabbed the attention of the average heathen, but that was really okay. Nothing he said sounded too crazy. I told him he was doing fine, though no-one was stopping to listen. He gave me a pamphlet with cheerfully entitled sections like: *You're A Sinner!* and *Jesus Loves You, Sinner!* And perhaps more appropriately: *Wash Yourself Clean (Of Your Sins)!*

So after work one day Jay Jay and Shafique sat down together to chat about things. Defuse the tension. I think they were ready for a row, both made up to be martyred there and then for their beliefs, if it came to that. But when they actually *talked,* they found that barring minor dogmas, they basically agreed on everything. The Great Debate lasted all of five minutes before they were stunned into silence while they processed things. And thereafter it was like they'd covered that topic - time to move on. Since then they get on fantastically well. They even call each other Brother. Where did all this religious tolerance come from? Nestor and I were expecting jihad by the jukebox.

Sitting in the pub window, and half-listening to Nestor, Shafique and Jay Jay idly play an imaginary game of *Wash!* with the passing cars.

About *Wash!.* I should explain. To keep up levels of interest at work (washing cars, you may be surprised to learn, can occasionally get tedious) there's a competition going on between the four teams. It has the most intricate set of rules you could imagine, I swear they're completely beyond comprehension.

The basic principle is that your team scores points for every car washed. This all started last year. Before that there had been a regular gambling cartel operating among the washers for some time – simply because it's something to do – betting on cars, nothing too serious, just which colour car was going to be next through the entrance, that kind of thing. Not much money involved.

At least to begin with. Competitive gambling among very bored people does tend to spiral. So the money involved crept up until one day an Ethiopian lad bet his entire season's earnings on red, it came up black, and he ended up being deported. Harry cracked right down.

For a while they tried to continue the whole betting thing except without any money. Playing for pride. But the thrill had gone, so at the start of this season a few of the guys put their heads together – I think Shafique and Shireen were

principal instigators – and came up with a new game, *Wash!*,
whereby each car washed scores according to make, model
and colour. Almost straightforward, if you can remember
the scoring system.

But then there are two sets of bonus scores. The first
set corresponds to time and place bonuses, for example:
anything washed on Tuesday between 3 and 5 in the
afternoon (a notoriously quiet time) scores double. And
anything washed with no cars on either side of it scores at
two thirds (with one or two exceptions). The second set of
bonuses are car-related: the number of passengers in the
car, what you can see on the back seat, that kind of thing.
All these bonuses intersect and some take precedence over
the others, just don't ask me which.

My life outside the job is completely taken up with
learning the rules. I sit and wait for the bus and tot up the
scores of the cars going by. I watch out of my window at
the cars on the street below and do the maths. It doesn't
make any sense to me at all. I don't even know what the
numbers mean.

"What do you mean, mean?" says Shafique. "They're
just numbers. They don't mean anything."

Even when the final scores are in at the start of the next
day I don't know who's won until someone tells me.

"Mother of God," Shafique sighs. "It's so simple. Just let
me score for you today, alright?"

He explains again, and it doesn't make any sense.

Although no-one writes anything down, everyone apart
from me seems to be entirely able to keep their own score
at the same time as keeping tabs on everyone else's. At the
end of the days there are no arguments. These guys are not
unsmart. Why they're washing cars and not doing particle
physics is beyond me. Some university somewhere must see
the potential and start handing out scholarships.

"Okay. 16:5:24."

"No. 24? No. I mean, how? *Seventeen.*"

"Why is that seventeen?"

"Allah preserve us. A red 2001 Mondeo with an empty space on either side? With a baby-seat? At eleven o'clock? Are you stupid man? Minus seven. You see?"

Harry has definitely noticed that something's going on, and after the gambling debacle he's keeping a close eye on us, but he hasn't yet twigged quite what's happening. I'm not entirely surprised.

Finally, after our fourth round – four beers and twelve cokes, though the cokes are small because they only have those pikey little bottles – Harry comes in. He looks like he's been waiting out in the rain. His shirt is soaked, only the garish colours keeping it from being see-through, and his Bermuda shorts are dripping. He looks uncharacteristically worried.

"Hi Harry," I say.

"You could have left a note or something," he says. "We need to go."

"Sorry Harry," we say.

"Where are we going, Harry?" asks Nestor cheerily. There's an edge of excitement to his voice from too much caffeine.

"Cleaning job," Harry says.

We pile outside and in to a waiting car. Out of habit, and despite being the smallest, Nestor baggsies the front seat. Disturbingly, given his distaste for cars, Harry gets in the driver's seat. I didn't even know he could drive. Shafique, Jay Jay and I cosy up in the back.

With a spine-arresting crunch Harry throws the car into first gear and we make a sharp jerk forwards, then pull away at a speed which presses us back hard into the seats.

As soon as the g-force lessens off there's the sound of four sets of seatbelts clicking swiftly into place.

WE HEAD SOUTH East, I reckon. More or less. Pretty soon I don't know where we are. I've lived in London my whole life and most of the city is still a mystery to me – a mile from my home in the wrong direction and nothing looks familiar, except that it all looks a bit like South London. Grey and rained-on. It all looks a bit like home.

We drive for a long time. The streets edge by. Living in one neighbourhood you forget how big the city is, it goes on for mile after mile. And watching the houses go by I get the same thought I always get when I'm somewhere new, something I've never quite understood, nor how it makes me feel, the idea that this patch of land here, that yard – it's all somebody's home. It may be an outlying blip on my radar, but it's dead-centre on someone else's. It all means something to somebody.

At least it's a distraction. Inside the car we're all getting a little edgy, not least because of our heightened appreciation of a certain salient statistic here – that the longer we spend in the car with Harry driving, the more likely we are to die young.

He seems to know where we're going, though, driving relentlessly on. Out the window the suburbs begin to blur into uniformity. It all looks quite pleasant, though, not a bad place to live, despite the rain.

Eventually the terraced housing thins out, we take a right turn onto a rough road and enter what looks to be a disused industrial estate. Broken piles of old bricks line the pot-holed drive. There are scattered large buildings, each with an immaculate collection of broken windows. The concrete turning areas are grown over with thick grass.

At the end of the lot, fenced off by a suspiciously tall

and professional-looking piece of barbed-wire technology, there's a big old brick power station. Harry drives up to the fence where it runs across the track and toots his horn. We wait. From where I'm squished between Jay Jay and the door, looking along the wire fence, I can see that at the top of every other post there's a security camera. A red light on each one gives an understated, intermittent flash. It may be an optical illusion caused by the blurred light and blowing rain, but they all appear to be focused on us.

Then the section of the fence that's directly in front of us slides soundlessly aside. Harry stays where he is. Nestor looks across at him, with a well, boss? look. Harry has long since ceased like he looks like he knows what he's doing, which is worrying for the rest of us. But he re-starts the car on only the second attempt and shuffles it forward, juggling painfully through the low gears until we jerk to a halt outside the power station itself.

We get out – the rain has lost heart a little, let up – and wander into the disused power station. There's a great gap in the wall where presumably a door once swung. The building is a cathedral of space, a wire-frame draft of a past coliseum. It's really quite impressive. And considering that there's no roof, the interior is remarkably clean. I'm worrying about the deficiency of empty cans of lager and piss-stains, until I remember about the fence. The concrete floor is solid-looking, and brushed clean. There's a raised section bang in the middle, with a hatch door in the centre of that. It looks like the top of a submarine. It's funny how some of the most interesting things in your life happen when you're drunk. It seems such a waste.

"Here we are," says Harry, looking relieved. "Someone'll be along soon."

"See you later then," he adds.

We give him a hurt look.

"I have to collect the money," he offers, by way of explanation. "I'll pick you up," he says.

Then he's out of the building, in his car and driving away, surprisingly smoothly, by the sounds, and very quickly too.

"You live in a very strange country," Nestor says to me when he's gone. "Strange people," he adds, accusingly.

"Harry's Hawaiian," I say. "And you live here too."

We sit around on the raised concrete step beside the hatch, fold our arms and wait. The drizzle drifts on down.

With a metallic edge to it, and making us all jump, a loud voice suddenly vents from a hidden speaker.

"Please lift the hatch and descend the ladder," it says.

Shafique is holding his heart, taking deep breaths of air, pretending to have an attack. Nestor giggles.

"Please lift the hatch and descend the ladder," the voice repeats. It sounds authoritative enough.

We assume it means us, so we stand up. Jay Jay leans forward and with a bit of effort levers up the heavy hatch.

"There's a ladder," he says, looking down. He sounds almost surprised. "Do we go in?"

"After you," says Nestor.

One by one we get a hold of the top of the ladder and start climbing down the tube. It's a long way. We climb in unison, to a vertical marching beat, our shoes making a pleasing rhythmic clang on the metal rungs.

"Please seal the hatch behind you," the voice says. Nestor, last in, seals the hatch above him.

At the bottom of the ladder is a corridor, modern and narrow, but tastefully brightened with some well-concealed wall lighting. We wander along until we find a door on the left. There is a note pinned to it. After the impressive trick with the voice and the hidden speakers, this comes across as a little cheap.

Dear Cleaners,

Please enter the changing rooms and put on the protective equipment. Enter the main hall through the big doors. After you have finished, please leave all the equipment as you found it and return the way you came. Thank you.

Yours, etc.

PS Make sure all doors are PROPERLY shut as you go through them.

BEYOND THE DOOR the changing rooms are fairly standard. A wall of lockers for our things, a shower area, rows of benches with pegs. Hanging on the pegs, dazzlingly bright yellow, are what look to be four chemical warfare suits.

We examine them suspiciously for a while, then realise there's not much else to do. We strip down to underwear and t-shirts, stowing our jackets, shoes and waterproofs in the lockers. I struggle into the contamination suit. Your feet go into the boots, and the rest peels up around you, it's an unpleasantly plastic and sticky feeling. There's a hood with a built in visor-and-gas-mask arrangement which flips down and seals to the front. I centre the visor, look at the ridiculous figures of my costumed colleagues. Nestor looks like a little banana. We laugh at each other, then go to look for the big doors, which we find further down the corridor.

They open through into an immense hall. It looks like an aircraft hangar – big enough for sure, though perhaps a little further underground than is usual – a roof which raises in the centre, an even bigger set of doors at the far end. Huge spotlight beams in the roof, glaring down. And parked in the middle of the huge warehouse space is a massive red tanker. It's the largest truck I've ever seen in my life and it still looks like a toy car lost in a garage. The number plates have been blacked out. Beside us, against the wall, lean four long-handled brushes, and coiled beside them is a hose.

On closer inspection the tanker is not actually red, merely coated in dirt, filthy with a thick crimson dust which seems impacted onto the surface. I stroke a gloved finger over it and it doesn't come away, just leaves a garish blood-like stain on my suit. This looks like hard work. No wonder Harry pissed off.

Nestor closes the big doors and finds a tap where he can hook up the hose. It's a neat device, trigger-operated at the spray end, a high-pressure affair designed to simply blast dirt from the target.

We get to work. Nestor jets the water, which slices into the layer of dirt, and we try and brush it off. He's really enjoying himself. Red mud streams from the surface of the tanker and coagulates round our sewn-in rubber boots. It's hot work while wearing the suits, but with a bit of application, the stuff actually starts to come off. Pretty soon we're covered in it.

"I worked in an abattoir once," says Nestor, conversationally. "It was a lot like this."

The brushing takes quite a while. Long enough for me to sober up.

"So how many points for this thing?" I ask, half-way through.

Shafique puts down his brush and leans on it. Behind his mask I can see him working it out.

"Never mind," I say quickly. Sometimes they really take *Wash!* too seriously.

Eventually we're done. Nestor finally hoses the last of the stubborn mud into the floor drains. We even brushed clean the tyre tracks – might as well be thorough, after all – and so, quietly proud, we stand back and admire our work. The tanker, it turns out, is a sparkling new silver, unmarred by company logo. It gleams in the bright lights. We wash off the brushes, put everything back where we found it, and leaving the tanker behind us, shut the big doors on it.

Still in our suits we get under the showers. It's a strange feeling. Not really pleasurable, because you can't feel the water, but you get a certain weird satisfaction that you won't have to dry yourself afterwards. Except after we've stripped off the suits we get back under the showers to wash away all the sweat, and it's only after we've done that we realise we haven't been provided with any towels.

Dressed again, but still damp, we hang the contamination suits back up on the pegs. Then closing the doors behind us we walk back along the corridor, climb with aching arms the ladder, and open the hatch. There's a slight whoosh of escaping air as the seal breaches. We come up into the power station. It's already dark. And very quiet. The rain seems to have cleared up, though. The air is blissfully cool, but with our damp clothes it gets a little cold in no time.

There's no voice at the top, telling us what to do, so we shut the hatch behind us, and stand a moment in the middle of the skeleton building, roofed by clouds, purple in the night. Then we head towards the entrance.

The empty night cracks a grin at us.

"Where's our lift man?" asks Nestor. "Are we supposed to walk home or what?"

Seeing as the power station provides no actual shelter, we decide to go wait at the road turning. We worry for a while how we'll get through the fence, but find it half open, as though the power on the door had given out. The cameras hang a little limply on their posts. We exit and make a tired walk through the rest of the site.

As we come back out onto the road proper it starts raining with a youthfully renewed enthusiasm. Shafique takes one look at the clouds and says what he always says when it rains.

"You know they should never have built this country underwater. In Nigeria now it is sunny."

We ignore him. It would be night-time in Nigeria, too.

It's strangely quiet around. There's an odd smell in the air, perhaps marking the demise of a distant drain.

Time passes. We get wetter. There's still no sign of Harry.

"Sod this," I say. "Let's go get a bus." There's a general agreement from the others, so we go off in search of one.

Eventually we reach a main street and find a bus shelter to shiver under. The stream of water gathering pace along the street comes up to our ankles, so we balance on the uncomfortable benches. We wait for a bus, but it doesn't show. Unusually for London, not even the wrong-numbered bus turns up. Not even a car goes by. It's like everything got washed away in the rain. For a fleeting moment, and for the first time in my life, I wish I had my own car. Or boat. A boat would do fine.

"It's like with Noah," says Jay Jay.

"I noah what you mean." I say.

But he's too busy scanning the sky. I follow his gaze. Just clouds, rain.

"What are you looking for?" I ask.

"Jesus," he says.

"Yeah," I say. "Amazing rain."

He looks at me, confused.

ACTUALLY, THE WATER is starting to get seriously deep.

Shafique takes out his phone card and wades over to a phone box to try and get us a taxi.

"See if you can get a water taxi," advises Nestor.

"No answer," Shafique says when he gets back. "At this time of night they're never going to come this far south of the river anyway."

We have a brief discussion about the possibility of stealing a car, which is ended by the realisation that even if we could find one, none of us know how to drive, never mind hotwire it. So with our options running out, and tired though we are, we decide to slosh back along to the supermarket by ourselves.

We follow the signposts for central London. It takes us a good few hours, an exhausting slog along slick, amber streets. In places it looks more like Venice. The rain keeps raining. *I could do this all day, no worries,* it seems to be saying cheerily.

I keep myself happy by thinking of Shireen, and wishing I'd brought her umbrella along. Then I get to wondering how my mum's doing. She'll have been up wondering why I'm so late home. I don't usually stay out.

There's the first sign of dawn in the sky, the light merging weirdly with that of the street lamps, an almost tangible glow in the streets. Thoroughly worn out we roll up at the supermarket.

Which is open, though no one's there. The rain has started to wash in beneath the automatic doors. The checkouts are unmanned, and there are abandoned baskets of groceries in the aisles. The car park is half-full of parked-up cars, but entirely empty of people. The drains here seem to be working a bit better, or it's not been raining so much here, because the water over the tarmac is a good deal shallower, there are islands of protruding dry land created by the warped surface. We poke around for a few minutes, but nothing turns up. I decide I don't want to be here. I want to find Shireen and take her home for tea, introduce her to my mum.

"I'm off to my mum's place," I say. Even if everyone else in the world has disappeared off somewhere, my mum's the sort of person who'll still be in, the kettle on.

"Me too," says Shafique. He's joking. His mum lives in Africa.

But he stays standing beside me. And Jay Jay sidles up too, making it clear we're not going without him.

"Nestor?" I say.

He has a think. "I'm going to stay," he says. "Wash some cars, you know?"

He sounds quite positive about it, so I nod in encouragement. He heads off to get our trolley and we stand there a while and watch him.

For a moment I get a nervous feeling building up in my chest, so I take some deep breaths, wait for it to pass. It's something I used to get a lot. A fear of the future (or *for* it). Panic attacks if I went too far from home, stuff like that. It can really get to you. So the trick, I learned, is to not let it penetrate, to imagine it just washing off – water from a duck's back, and all that. If you have to stay home, stay home. *Don't let it get to you*, has been my philosophy since. Somehow I stopped worrying about those things. Never quite moved out of my mum's place, but we have a good relationship, and renting a place is expensive, so that never seemed like a bad thing. I settled for happiness in the things I had, left the future to look after itself. After all, as my doctor liked to ask me, rhetorically, what's the worst that could happen? I remind myself of this. The nervous feeling goes and I perk up a little.

We push off. The rain thickens again like someone threw open a heavenly tap, so we pull off our fluorescent jackets, and hold them over our heads to create makeshift umbrellas. It doesn't really help.

Ahead of us the streets are empty. There's really nobody around. Just Nestor, there behind us in the depopulated car park, determined to get some *Wash!* points on the board, pushing his water trolley down the rows, the green hose sidewinding along behind him through the puddles. He's washing every car left in the place, one at a time, a huge smile of satisfaction on his exhausted face.

Julia Bell

Urdd Gobaith Cymry

JANET WATCHED AS his car backed away down the uneven track and secretly stuck her fingers up at the driver. His face was twisted away from her, looking over his shoulder as he turned the car into the road where the tatty sign with the red green and white triangle was shedding paint like dandruff into the weeds. All the way down there in the car, through the endless landscape of soggy green fields dotted with clumps of depressed-looking sheep, she had sat with her arms folded, ignoring his deliberately cheerful whistling and inane comments about the weather. Just because her mother was in love with him, didn't mean she had to go there too.

It started with weekends. Off to some unpronounceable village halfway up a mountain, with Geraint the jolly new boyfriend who made her mother flustered and embarrassed and not at all like the woman who had walked out on Dad. Janet was relegated to the back seat with Lisa who complained because she wanted to be back home where it was warm and there was a colour TV. Janet just watched in horror as her Mother fell in love with this ugly landmark of a man who had ruddy cheeks and muddy boots and spoke in a language that sounded like he was trying to cough up phlegm, and there was nothing she could do to stop it.

Since they moved it had pretty much been an all out war. She hadn't spoken to her mother properly in months, communication reduced to sniping at the breakfast table and staring at each other over dinner. Janet had recently discovered that refusing to eat anything her mother cooked in Geraint's grotty 70s kitchen was proving to be quite effective. She'd lost nearly a stone since they'd moved in, and last Sunday her mother had left the room in tears after Janet sat impassively, staring at the steaming joint of lamb and all the trimmings refusing to talk or eat, or act like there was anyone else in the room. "I don't see why you can't just be *happy* for me."

It was his idea to send her to the centre. "Help her settle in, like."

Urdd Gobaith Cymry – as far as Janet knew it meant something like 'the club that is the hope of Wales'. A kind of Welsh Summer Camp, where, according to the inky leaflet, they got to do trekking and horse riding and swimming and water polo; all in Welsh.

"Sounds crap." She'd said, pushing past him to go upstairs. He'd cleared out the attic for her, the walls of which she'd pretty much covered up already with pictures of Robert Smith and Boy George.

But saying that had been a mistake, it just meant that her mother signed her up for it the very next day.

A LUMPY WOMAN in a brown tracksuit and chipped clipboard puffs her way up the steps. The turn-in is a mossy concrete semi-circle which sits on the cliff above the centre.

"Janet Jones?"

"Er, no, it's Brown, actually."

The woman looks confused, drawing her lips back across her teeth to make her mouth look like a rictus, like something almost pornographic. Janet has to look away. "It says Jones here."

"That's my mother's *new* name. *My* name is Janet *Brown*." Janet speaks really slow in case the woman can't understand her. Round here it's really Welsh, so Welsh that there are still old people alive who can't speak any English. Janet can't understand this, that in 1984, at the pinnacle of the modern age, there are still people in Britain who can't speak English.

"OK then, right you are. Come along now. Everyone else is in the barn doing Orientation. You can find your room later, I'm afraid that all the best beds will be gone by now. You're late."

"I missed the bus." Which was why Geraint had to drive her down here. She hadn't so much missed the bus, as sat there at the bus stop while the bus pulled in and then sat there watching as it pulled out again. She waited another twenty minutes and then walked back to the house. Her mother had gone crazy, mainly, Janet knew, because she'd walked in on them kissing.

"I don't want to see you! I don't want to see you!" She'd shouted, fumbling as she buttoned up her blouse. "Why haven't you gone *away?*"

ORIENTATION IS IN the barn, a corrugated farm building, inside Janet can hear the piano, they're already singing. There is a lot of singing in Wales. The room is muggy and smells of damp coats and sweaty feet. There are no seats at the back so she has to climb over the legs and bags to get to an empty seat, a front one, that is at an awkward angle to the cheap plasterboard stage. So far she had learned make out two phrases in the hash mess of sounds. *Sit udach chi?* (How are you?) and *Dewch umlan* (come along). The teacher who greets her says neither of these things so she smiles blankly at him.

"Sorry, *bach*," he repeats in English. "I asked you for your name."

"Janet." She says, sure she could light a match off her cheeks.

"Well *Croeso* Janet!" He grins at her through a hairy beard. "I'm Mr Puw, but you can call me Barry, because we're all friends here, but you'll have to pick up the lingo as we go along. We have an English Not policy here I'm afraid." And he rattles off something in Welsh to which everyone claps.

Janet knows about Welsh Not. It's the first thing they taught her in Remedial Welsh. When the English set up the state education system they banned the children from speaking Welsh in the playground, and would punish them by making them wear a sign around their necks that read Welsh Not. The last person wearing the Welsh Not would be caned at the end of the day. The teacher's voice was still hot with injustice when she told the class this story.

After another song, which Mr Puw brings up on the overhead projector, pointing at the words line by line with a pencil, they are put into activity groups. Janet is in the swimming group along with a collection of other girls, all with bad haircuts and ruddy cheeks. She thinks she can smell cowshit on one of them. The boys are going riding and orienteering. Janet keeps to herself, as they all traipse out to one of the outbuildings, what looks like a giant barn where there is a swimming pool. They are all talking in Welsh so it's easy to ignore them.

Their teacher in Miss Parry who is twenty two and doing her teacher training in Aberystwyth. She sidles up to Janet and asks her if she's OK.

"Yeah." Janet says. "Diolch yn fawr."

"Good girl."

But Janet detects weakness in Miss Parry. Her heavy make up is starting to spoil, her eyeliner sunk under her eyes. She's a student, not even a proper teacher.

The pool is small and slimy. There is a scum of green algae at the bottom and the tiles around the pool are loose. One of the girls trips and nearly falls in which makes everyone laugh. But Janet doesn't see what's so funny. She is indignant. The place is obviously a complete shithole.

"I'm not swimming in *that*." She says, pointing at the water. "It's disgusting."

There are murmurs of assent. "Yeah, Miss, it's gone green on the bottom!" They are talking English now. Janet smiles inwardly, as the teacher tries to stem the protest by shouting even louder in Welsh. But Janet can tell that Miss Parry thinks it's disgusting too. So in the end there is a kind of truce and they all shuffle out again into the drizzle to play netball instead.

Janet's protests have won her some respect. A girl called Mair introduces herself.

"It's crap here isn't it?" She says.

"Yeah."

They both refuse to play netball.

"I can't miss, I twisted my ankle."

"Miss I didn't bring any training shoes."

Miss Parry lets them sit it out on the wall by the turnaround. "Stay where I can see you. Are you sure you don't want to play? You'll have more fun."

But Janet doesn't want to have any fun. Since she got here, the slow, burning rage in her belly has become a blazing fire.

They are sleeping in dormitories, on cheap wooden bunks made of plasterboard. Eight in each room, with the top bunks so close to the ceiling you can touch the light bulb from the bed. Janet removes someone's bag and all their stuff and claims a top bunk for herself. She can see everything in the room from here and the cramped space makes her feel safe: if she had to she could hide up here.

All the others are in the hall doing more singing. She and Mair have told the teachers they needed a pee but they no intention of going back.

Mair takes the bed opposite and starts drawing on the wall with a biro.

"What are you writing?"

"Urdd is shit." Mair says.

Janet laughs and digs a biro out of her bag. She starts to scribble on the board of the bunk bed, deep and hard, a crosshatch of black lines. A shape starts to emerge out of the scribble, a hooded figure in a black robe. Janet is more deliberate now, outlining it, adding arms.

"What did they say this place used to be?" Janet asks.

"An old nunnery, or something, but then the church got burned down and then it was a farm, and now it's this place. That's what they were telling us before you came in."

Janet looks at her drawing and is pleased. She writes The Black Nun in spooky letters next to it and laughs.

"What have you done?" Mair comes up the ladder, gasping when she sees the extent of the damage. "Oh my God! That's so freaky!"

"Maybe we should spread the word."

By BEDTIME THE girls' dormitory is buzzing with gossip. The Black Nun has been seen, standing in one of the rooms. There are black marks on the walls and graffiti on he inside of every bunk bed that says Beware The Black Nun. The teachers are playing it down. They are angry about the damage, but they are sceptical about the stories.

Janet and Mair are delighted with the frenzy they have created, as two of the eldest girls there it has been easier than they thought to persuade the eleven and twelve year olds of the Ghost of the Black Nun who haunts the corridors of Urdd Camp at night. One of the eleven year olds thinks she has seen the nun in the mirror of the girl's bathroom and has been screaming and crying for ten minutes. Janet and Mair lie in their bunks stifling triumphant laughter.

"Oh God that's so funny."

"Did you see her face?!"

"I think she wet herself!"

But it takes hours to calm the dormitory down. As the giggles subside, Janet gets a headache and the burning bright of the light bulb isn't helping. But no one in the room wants to put the light out in case of the Black Nun.

In THE MORNING Janet is tired and cold. There is condensation on the inside of all the windows. At breakfast all the food is laid out in the dining room on a trestle table with fluorescent labels in Welsh and English there is *llaeth* (milk) and *uwd* (porridge), *bara* (bread), *menyn* (butter) *sugion oren* (orange juice). The porridge is as grey and pasty as the weather. Mair complains that she only got an hour's sleep. The teachers woke them up at seven because they're supposed to be doing *marchogaeth* (horse riding) this morning.

Janet sips on her *sugion oren* which is dark-coloured and acidic, and made up from powder that she saw Miss Parry mixing in the kitchen. She is quite looking forward to *marchogaeth*, although she doesn't want to admit it because that would mean she was properly participating. Like the pictures of happy Mr Urdd, the green white and red triangle man that is the logo of the camp and is painted around the walls of the dining room. The crude and inane expression on his face reminds her of Geraint and her mother and it puts her in a really bad mood.

Marchogaeth happens in another bigger barn. It smells of sawdust and fresh horse shit. They are given hard hats which they have to buckle up under the chin. Janet's is too big and drops down over her eyes, but she doesn't have time to complain before one of the teachers comes along talking at her in fast, incomprehensible Welsh and helps her mount a mangy looking piebald. Its mane is dirty and it smells of oils and sweat and strange un-nameable animal smells.

Janet adjusts herself in the saddle and tries to copy the teacher who is shouting at them in Welsh. Her horse lurches forward, jerking her backwards. She can't quite get her balance.

The horse has stopped now and Janet can't get it to go again. Everyone else is trotting gently round the ring, but her horse won't budge.

"Come on." She says, and then in Welsh: *"Dere'mlan."*

Someone's shouting at her now, but no amount of kicking or cajoling will get the bloody thing to move. She looks behind her to see that Mair is right behind, her horse so close she can almost pet its nose.

"It won't go." Janet says, helplessly.

"Kick it."

"I've *tried*."

But then, before anyone can do anything Mair's horse,

impatient to get things moving, neighs and tosses its head and then bites down hard on the rump of Janet's piebald nag.

Janet isn't quite sure what happens next, it's like a series of still frames. The horse rising up, with her clinging to the back, tilted so she can see the rust in the corrugated roof. Then tarmac and sky and the loud thunder of hooves. The horse galloping fast, and the saddle slipping like it isn't tied on properly. She can hear people shouting but she is too shocked to scream. They pass the Urdd Centre and on and on down the lane. Then there is a blue van coming towards them, and the horse isn't stopping and she is sure they are going to collide and she closes her eyes. Then suddenly they are in a field and before she knows it, finally, she lets go, and is thrown with a thump into the wet grass.

She lies there for what seems like ages, her hat askew, hands over her face. Winded, she makes strange crouping noises. When the teachers find her she is trembling and crying and asking for her mother.

Miss Parry has tied her arm in a sling. She doesn't think anything's broken, but Janet's wrist has started to throb and swell up.

"We've called your mother." Miss Parry says. "She's coming right away to take you to the hospital."

Janet is pleased about this fact, in spite of herself. Miss Parry has made her a sweet cup of tea for the shock and given her some painkillers for her arm.

"I don't know what happened to that horse." Miss Parry looks at Janet curiously. "It got spooked by something."

"Yes." Janet sips her tea still feeling woozy and kind of sick, Miss Parry seems very far away.

"Perhaps it was *Y Lleian Du?*"

"Eh?"

She is sure Miss Parry is smiling. "Work it out."

Janet wonders what her mother will think when she gets here and sees the state of this place. Perhaps she will realise what a mistake all this Welshie nonsense is and they can go back to Birmingham and have their old life back. But this thought no longer gives her the comfort that it once did, and what she wants more than anything just now is armistice, an end to the war. The throbbing pain in her arm is worsening, turning sharp. She's sure she has broken it, whatever Miss Parry says. And in a funny way she's glad of it. She knows that her mother will feel really bad about this, and that is enough, for now. Her old life is suddenly very far away from this craggy place with its strange consonants and singing, so far away, that she has almost forgotten what it is she has been fighting for.

"Y Lleian Du? Is that the Black Nun? In Welsh?"

Miss Parry laughs. "You got it kiddo."

"Can you write it down for me?"

THE CENTRE GOT closed down a few years later. Something to do with health and safety. But anyone who went there when it was still open could probably find, if they looked, *Yma Y Lleian Du!* hurriedly scrawled on the skirting board of the administrators office with a regulation green Urdd Gobaith Cymry promotional pen.

CLARA WIGFALL
The Ocularist's Wife

16th of July, 1870, Paris

THERE IS A certain point in the day, late afternoon – the exact hour dependent upon the season – when, if the sun might happen to shine, the walls of Monsieur Hervé P. Pontellier's establishment light up iridescent. Those small orbs that line each shelf are set aglow and the very air is shot with jewel-like colour. Sitting at his desk, Monsieur Pontellier will lift his head and pause. Across his face, the rainbow shimmer of a live trout slipping from the hands.

Passing in the corridor behind the shop, as she steps to retrieve a forgotten novel from the garden, the glowing rectangle of light pulls at Madame Pontellier's attention.

She turns her head, the tendons in her pale neck curving smoothly into line with her shoulder blade. The corridor is dark and the tunnelled effect of the lighted doorway in the distance reminds her of looking down a child's kaleidoscope, the way the colours slot gently back and forth amongst themselves like dancers on a ballroom floor. Softly, her weight rests back upon the silken heels of her slippers, feet still paced apart on the tiles.

Her husband's back is angled from her while his face, raised to bask in the light, is held in profile.

He is a large man, Monsieur Pontellier, a man whose knees graze the underside of his desktop. He carries his size awkwardly, as if it embarrasses him somewhat. Standing upright, his head hangs forward a little, shoulders droop backwards, legs are loosely angled at the knee. He almost has the concertina profile of someone seen in a fairground mirror. The distorted glass has further stretched his facial features too, for forehead and chin recede backwards behind the length of his nose, their diagonals hampered only by the sweep of his hairline and the jut of his Adam's apple. He has no chin to speak of. Keeping his arms close at his sides, his tread is careful, like one walking anxious through a tightly packed china shop. He gives the appearance of a man constantly wary of clumsy movement, which is strange, because Monsieur Pontellier is by nature extremely precise.

The bell at the door breaks his contemplation.

"Ah ha," says his visitor, gesturing towards those luminous spheres surrounding them, "the eyes of heaven look upon us today!"

Pontellier chuckles, "Afternoon, Courtois."

"Good afternoon to you, too," says Courtois, taking a seat at the desk, his feet lifting to perch on the stool's rungs. "Spectacular, ha, quite spectacular," he revolves his head in the tinted light. "You could charge a franc entry to see this, my friend."

"I daresay. And how does the day treat you, Courtois?"

"Oh, quite fine, quite fine. The marmoset is pregnant."

"The marmoset?" Pontellier cocks his head.

"The marmoset, indeed. Quite a coup. Terribly difficult to breed in captivity." He crosses one leg over the other then studies a skim of dirt lodged beneath his fingernails.

"I see, yes I see." Pontellier is working while he talks. Fashioning a perfect pupil, flecking pale threads of paint across an azure iris.

He has known Courtois, the city zookeeper, since their schooldays. Still remembers him a boy with eager voles in his pockets and newts squirming in his handkerchief.

Perhaps because his career has indulged his childhood passion, Courtois has retained a youthfulness of appearance. His skin still blooms pink at the cheeks and his hair is parted neatly and combed flat as if by an attentive matriarch. He has an endearing habit of blinking his eyelids rapidly, a quiver of lash beneath the thick lenses of his spectacles. There are always, to his great irritation, short mammalian hairs caught in the wool of his suits which even persistent brushing seems unable to remove. His appearance is otherwise meticulous.

Before Pontellier, Courtois assumes a languid air of articulate confidence, but it is a quality he finds himself unable to reproduce before other men. "Lord, what heat," he sighs, drawing a mustard-coloured handkerchief from his pocket (no newts these days) and wiping it across his forehead. "I suppose you've read the newspaper?"

Squinting at his brush strokes, Pontellier's response is

solemn. "They're goading us with that dispatch."

"My view exactly."

"And I've a fear we might take the bait." He worries at his lower lip a moment and draws in a deep breath, his nostrils flaring. "Lord help us if we do, that's all I can say."

"Lord help us? You don't think we'd win?" All of a sudden, Courtois's attention is distracted by a slight movement in the corner and he stumbles to his feet. "Madame Pontellier," he says politely, dipping his head, the brilliantine upon his hair glinting in her direction.

Madame Pontellier has the pale constitution of a woman in the early stages of consumption. The disease is merely nibbling at present, gnawing slightly from within; so quiet that it goes as yet undetected, mistaken for that only vaguely unhealthy apathy not irregularly the preserve of well-bred young ladies with time on their hands. She spends the afternoons reclining upon the chaise longue, a romance splayed at her side, the pages barely turned, her eyelids fluttering weakly at the edges of sleep. The maid treads quietly so as not to disturb her mistress, removes a cup of tepid tea, careful not to let the cup rattle in the saucer, and thinks to herself, "Why, no wonder she lacks colour."

Madame Pontellier stands now in the doorway, very slightly off centre, her gaze level. She is the colour of porcelain. With a faint nod, she acknowledges Courtois.

"Supper, Hervé," she says. "If you'll come up now to wash, please." She slides her eyes back to the zookeeper. "Good evening, Monsieur Courtois," and bows her head a fraction.

The two men are silent as she turns, listening to the dry whisper of her skirts against the tiles.

Courtois draws in his breath with a faint sucking sound, "Madame calls. I'd better let you go, heh?" He is still fumbling with his hat brim, feigning jocularity. "Until tomorrow?"

"Until tomorrow." Pontellier watches his friend leave and notices that the evening sun has passed. His shop has submerged once again in dusty shade and those false eyes lining the walls are cold and hard.

20th of July, 1870

KNOWING THAT HIS friend doesn't step out until lunchtime to buy the daily newspaper, Courtois denies himself his morning coffee to pay a fleeting visit to Pontellier's shop. He walks the streets briskly in the early sun, the news folded beneath his arm, perspiration causing the print to smudge against his jacket front. But it is not Monsieur Pontellier whom he finds behind the counter when he pushes open the door but Madame.

She is sitting in her husband's chair, idly flicking through a fashion journal laid on the desk before her. She looks up when Courtois enters and arches her eyebrows. "Monsieur Courtois, what brings you here so early?"

Courtois has come to a surprised halt before the desk. He drops his head and finds himself looking at the widespread page of her magazine. Pen and ink renderings of women's corsetry, the models cut below the torso, trussed at the bosom, beribboned, their backs arching, their lips open slightly as if the garments leave them silently gasping for breath. Madame Pontellier's gaze drops with his, stares flatly at the fashion spread, lifts again. "Can I help you, Monsieur Courtois?"

He falters, "I was looking for…"

"Hervé's out back, blowing glass." She gestures towards

the rear of the house. "Of course, I could disturb him for you."

Her voice, thinks Courtois, is like spilt liquid creeping across floorboards. He feels obliged to decline her offer, assuring her instead that, "Oh no, no, it's nothing important. Certainly nothing of any urgency." And then, adding almost as an afterthought, "Only, perhaps you might be so kind as to ensure that he sees this," and he thrusts the creased and sweaty newspaper across the countertop.

As he finishes, the door opens behind him. Courtois swivels his body towards the entering customer with palpable relief: a corpulent gentleman with a black felt eyepatch, the arrival of whom provides the necessary distraction for Courtois to take his leave without ceremony.

The gentleman approaches the counter, wheezing in the heat, and leans towards Madame Pontellier. "Morning, Madame." He is a fleshy-lipped man of ruddy complexion. "Cecil Bouillot. I was having an eye custom-made." A fleck of spittle lands upon the newspaper lying between them. "Would it be ready for collection, do you know?"

With a neat movement, Madame Pontellier closes the page of her magazine upon Courtois's paper and sweeps it aside.

"Bouillot? One moment." A row of small brown paper envelopes is pinned against the wall, their lower halves each a pregnant bulge beneath a pencilled name. Madame Pontellier runs her finger along the line, reciting the names as she does so. "Guyot-Clement, Courtillon, Ducasse...Bouillot." She pinches the pin from the wall and tips out the contents of the envelope. "Monsieur, if you please," she says politely, lifting her hand before him. Bouillot squints his good eye at the glassy replica lying still in Madame Pontellier's palm. With a tremor, his fat lips lift into a smile.

"Ah, Madame." He exhales slowly. "Incredible! Your husband is a genius."

Madame Pontellier reaches the fingers of her other hand to play at the corner of her mouth.

"May I?" questions Bouillot, reaching already like a child for a bonbon. He twists the little sphere between his heavy fingers. "May I try it?"

Before she can nod assent, he has flipped back the eyepatch to reveal a pinkened clump of flesh bunched about a dark cavity. A small muscle in disarray causes the tissue to jerk rapidly as if alive. Bouillot pops the orb into the hollow, smiles with satisfaction to feel how the skin suckers close about the cool glass.

Like a greedy sea anemone, thinks Madame Pontellier, her stomach curdling faintly with distaste.

She hands a small mirror across to him and watches as he fingers the glass surface of the eye to align the iris with its azure counterpart. The muscle beneath the glassy curve still twitches erratically. "Fantastic, ha. Quite fantastic. A remarkable match, don't you think, Madame?" asks Monsieur Bouillot without turning from the mirror.

Bouillot departs shortly, leaving congratulations for Monsieur Pontellier, money for the cash till, and a black felt eyepatch for the wastebasket. As the shop door springs closed behind him, Madame Pontellier drops back into her husband's seat and draws her hands up to cover her face, her fingertips pressing against her closed eyelids. She remains like this for several moments before taking a deep breath and blinking her eyes open, then reaches for her magazine and slides it across the countertop. Opening it, her gaze falls on Courtois' newspaper. She turns it to read the headline: *FRANCE DECLARES WAR.* Her eyes scan the cover article slowly, a frown creasing her forehead, until Madame Pontellier's head lifts and she finds herself lost in a memory of a spring holiday she once took in Prussia as a child.

6th of September, 1870

MONSIEUR PONTELLIER LIKES his meat rare. Likes to take a slice into his tournedos and watch the blood ooze colour into the pale of the pepper sauce. Likes to taste the animal in what he eats. And he needs this now, needs a delight in something simple to divert his attention.

They are seated at the dining table, Pontellier in his house slippers, his shirt collar loosened. The blinds have been drawn to shield the afternoon sun and it is almost dark in the room but for fine slants of light that eke below the tasselled trim. The air is stuffy. Madame Pontellier sits across the table from her husband, dressed in light green silk, the colour reflecting dully upon her cheekbones. Her dark hair is pulled sharply back from her face and pinned neatly in place by an ivory comb. She is breathing via quick shallow breaths through her mouth, her eyes flickering about the room, darting past her husband's form so as she shan't catch his gaze should he look up.

"An excellent piece of beef, my dear," he declares finally, wiping his napkin across his mouth. Reaching for his newspaper, he shakes it open before him. Feels once again the slight stirring within him of a sensation akin - he can't deny it - to nervous exhilaration. Pontellier knows already of exactly what he will read; current events have become too precipitate to wait until lunchtime. Each one of his morning's customers has entered with the news skittering on their lips, wanting to discuss and argue, needing words to give shape to reality. The city is alive with the changes taking place around and within it, its consciousness heightened by the accelerated pace of all that is occurring – from another military defeat at war and the surrender of their emperor has come a bloodless revolution, the effortless overturning of an empire. So fast. In the moment before he begins to read, his glance lifts briefly above the page.

Madame Pontellier's eyes have fallen suddenly still. Her face has assumed an expression of composed lethargy. It is an expression her husband recognises with some weariness. Her plate is barely touched.

"Is something wrong?" He peers across his newspaper, features pointed with dutiful concern.

"I don't have an appetite," sighs Madame Pontellier, sliding the plate further from her.

Pontellier hesitates, wondering whether he should pass around the table to put an arm about her, decides against it. "Are you sickening?" He lowers his paper. "You have been looking a trifle peaky of late. Should we call the doctor perhaps?"

"Hervé, *no*..." her voice trails. "I simply haven't an appetite today. Do stop fussing." She rises from her seat, dropping her napkin against the tablecloth, and crosses to the chaise longue.

Monsieur Pontellier gazes awkwardly at the remains of her meal; the salad turning limp in the heat, the skin forming on the pepper sauce.

"Perhaps, perhaps a jargonelle." She speaks from beneath closed eyelids.

"A jargonelle? A *pear*, you mean?"

"A jargonelle," she sounds the word with accentuated precision.

"Of course," he sighs, "a jargonelle. I'll ask Claudine." He folds his paper and exits to find the maid. Without opening her eyes, Madame Pontellier begins to fan herself slowly with one hand. Her foot has fallen in a shaft of light and she curls it into the shadow back towards herself, kicking off the shoe as she does so and digging her stockinged heel into a cool crack in the upholstery. She waits like this for her husband to return. When he does he tells her, as she knew he would, that there aren't any jargonelles in the house. He'll step out to try and find one for her.

"Wait!" she cries, as he turns at the door. "Will you come here, please, Hervé?" He crosses and lowers himself beside her. She still has her eyes closed, but smiles a little, a slim smile, a smile that barely exerts, as he begins to stroke at her temple. "Do you love me?" she asks in a level voice.

Gently, he smoothes a stray lock of hair pressed against the damp of her brow.

"Let's go away..." her lips are dry, "...take a holiday."

"It's hardly the best of times for a holiday, my love." His hand has fallen still. The moment makes him feel suddenly awkward, too long of limb to be crouching like this.

"We could go to the Alps."

"Let's just wait and see, heh? See what happens with this war."

"That war, Hervé, it won't affect *us*, will it?" She frowns beneath his fingertips.

He pauses before continuing slowly, "No. No, my darling. We're sure to see victory any day now." He is glad she hasn't opened her eyes. In the dim light he studies her calm features, wondering if she can truly be that unaware of everything beyond herself. "Don't you worry," he says softly, 'this war shan't affect you in the least."

"Then I don't care to think on it."

Again, he is made to pause. A frown now smocks his brows as he observes her. "I'll fetch your jargonelle, my dear," he says abruptly. Leaning, he plants a kiss upon her cheek and has to halt himself from overbalancing.

She lies as she is until she hears the front door shut closed behind him, then wipes at her cheek with the back of her hand and rises. Her meal is still sitting on the table, the knife and fork pointing expectantly towards the rim of the plate. She lifts the meat between thin fingers and reaches her mouth towards it, careful not to let the sauce drip onto the silk of her dress. "My silly darling," she says aloud between mouthfuls. "Did I forget to tell you this isn't the season for jargonelles?"

11th of November, 1870

THE SCUFFLE OF wings is what awakens her; a pigeon has landed on the windowsill. Scratching the claws of one foot against the wood, it arcs its head back into its feathers, its bill reaching and teasing at some small parasite. A pitiful creature, skinny with dull matted feathers, gnarled legs deformed. The bird brings its head back up for air, bobbing its neck and shaking its wings again. Around the eyes, some disease has balded the skin to an angry pink.

"Shoo!" calls Madame Pontellier sharply, realising how long it is since she last saw a bird. The creature declines to stir. Irritated now, Madame Pontellier steps up from the chaise longue and across to the window, clapping her hands to make the pigeon flee. It spreads its wings and launches itself from the sill.

A lanky sallow-skinned youth has been watching the bird from the street. As it flies off he runs desperately after it, a hessian sack flapping in his hand. Madame Pontellier watches as the bird lifts into the white sky, then turns back to the drawing room. Her book has fallen face down onto the carpet but she doesn't reach to retrieve it, nor does she tidy the blanket which trails from the seat. The clock on the mantelpiece ticks with a quiet regularity.

"I'll go out," she says suddenly, speaking aloud into the empty room. "Yes, I'll go out," she says again, this time more firmly. And, having made the decision, she realises she must move herself quickly before lassitude overtakes once more. She strides through to the bedroom, the swirl of her skirts behind her disturbing the maid kneeling to polish the parquet. Claudine looks up, her neck craning to follow her mistress. She is surprised at such uncharacteristic haste.

"Something wrong, Madame?" she asks tentatively, leaning forward on her polishing rag to catch a better view.

She sees Madame Pontellier in front of the dressing table, hairpins clamped between her lips as she rearranges her hair. Lifting her chin upwards, she tilts her head from side to side, her eyes fixed on the looking glass. At one point she pauses and stares coldly at her own reflection, the intensity unsparing as if she is seeing for the first time a stranger and trying to memorise the face. A second later she stretches to reach for a hat perched on a mahogany stand behind her. It is a wide-brimmed raven-coloured affair, an ostrich feather bowing from the brim. Only now does she acknowledge Claudine.

"Lace my boots, please, Claudine."

"Of course, Madame," chimes the girl, scurrying up from her knees and smoothing her apron as she comes into the room. "The grey boots, Madame?"

Lowering her eyelids briefly in agreement, Madame Pontellier extends one foot towards the maid and rests back in her seat. And at that very moment it simply leaves her again, the desire to go out – how *comfortable* this little chair is – she actually feels it leaving, seeping from her toes into the pattern of the carpet, slipping from her fingers down the velvet arms of the chair. The recognition rankles. "How can you be so slow?" she asks irritably, ignoring the obvious hurry with which the girl is weaving the laces tight about the boot hooks.

"Is Madame going *out*?" queries Claudine as she ties the second lace, her tone somewhat incredulous.

And with that it is back, the yearning to leave the house, to escape the thick air of the drawing room. She sweeps up from her seat and steps fast from the room, her words crackling behind her, "Madame certainly is. Tell my husband, if you please, that I'll return before supper."

"Shouldn't I go with you?" calls Claudine hopelessly.

Seated back upon her heels, the maid watches her mistress' departure, follows the blood-red silk of her dress disappearing from the doorframe, and the last oily flash of that dandling ostrich feather.

"Well, I'll be..." she murmurs to herself and rises, rubbing at her stiff knees as she does so.

In the street, Madame Pontellier feels suddenly very alone, so unused is she to stepping out without a companion. It makes her strangely conscious of her physical being, of where her skin stops and the rest of the world begins. There are brittle autumn leaves caught at her feet which are sent whirling along the pavement by an impulsive squall of wind. She inhales the afternoon into her lungs, relishing the chill in the air, the hint of damp. Not that the day is altogether dull. The sky is papered with dense grey clouds but these are splitting at the seams like a piece of silk wearing thin and the late-afternoon light is easing through each snaking divide. It reflects against the glassy shopfronts, lighting them up like a row of teeth.

Madame Pontellier releases her breath slowly, then inhales again, her chest rising as she does so. Keeping her mouth tight, she lifts one hand and presses her palm against the doorframe, as if to test its solidity. Surprised at how the wood resists the pressure of flesh and bone, she releases the breath.

The colours are what catch at the corner of her eye. The lucidity of them. And turning, she sees her husband, seated at his work desk, surrounded by the glimmer of light through coloured glass. There is a quality of containment about the scene, framed as it is within the neat rectangle of his shop window, a neatly printed sign stating *Business as Usual* running like a subtitle along its lower half. It has a sense of composure, like a stage set for a ballet or the tiny perfection of a small room in a doll's house. Pontellier hasn't seen her. He is hunched over the wooden desktop, peering at a glass eyeball held between his fingertips. His brush moves like the tongue of a snake, quick darts that fleck the glass minutely. The movement is echoed subconsciously on his face in the twitching and pursing of his lips, the pleating of his brows.

There is something very charming in observing an individual so absorbed, so oblivious to anything beyond themselves. From her vantage in the street, Madame Pontellier feels the low thrill of the voyeur. She is transfixed.

How strange it is, that he should seem to her so utterly familiar and yet almost unrecognisable. When did the skin of his forehead begin the slow inching back of his hairline? When did those creases form around his eyes? She feels a sudden surge of warmth for her husband. A desire to take the curve of his head in her hands and kiss those shining expanses of skin at his temples. To rest her mouth a moment in the shallow dip of each eye socket, feeling the lashes batting like a moth beneath her lips. To trace the contours of his cheeks with the tip of her tongue.

And it is then that she notices: the glassy illumined eyes upon the walls are staring at her. Every single one of them. Staring fixedly in absolute silence.

With a gasp, Madame Pontellier turns and slams smack into an unexpected obstruction.

"Oh!" she cries. "Oh! Monsieur Courtois!"

"Madame Pontellier," he catches her shoulder to hold her upright, "whatever's wrong?"

"Oh, my," she lifts her hand to her neck and clutches at her collar. "Please, I'm quite fine. I…I was merely going to take a walk," she falters.

"A walk? Now? Alone?" There is a subtle hint of scorn underlying his bemusement.

"Yes," she says faintly.

"And Monsieur Pontellier knows about this? Madame, don't you realise that it's not *safe* for you to walk out alone? It could be dangerous, extremely dangerous. The city is under *siege*, Madame"

His manner surprises her more than his words, so used is she to his awkward reserve. And now that she looks at him, how curious, the man is almost transformed. Deep furrows have been drawn across his brow. Wan smudges swim beneath his heavy spectacle lenses where the skin below his eyes has puffed a shining mauve. His cheeks have lost their bloom, covered instead now by a rough shadow of stubble. His dark hair is in disarray.

She steps back from his hold. "You're quite right, Monsieur Courtois," she says carefully, "I don't know what I was thinking." Although she smiles, she feels a tightness in her chest, the resurfacing of an anxiety which, for a moment, she can't explain. "Come, let us go in together."

And as he steps to take her arm he dips his left hand, retrieving a brown-paper-wrapped package dropped in the collision. It has the limp quality of a butcher's parcel. She looks down briefly, but is distracted as they approach the shopfront. Confronted once again by those staring glass eyes, Madame Pontellier recalls suddenly the cause for her underlying sense of alarm.

14th of December, 1870

"PLEASE COME TO the table and eat, Mireille," pleads Monsieur Pontellier.

"A moment," Madame Pontellier says irritably, without turning from the window.

Outside, the snow is falling thickly, veiling the small procession trailing below in the street. There are five figures in the party. Slow-moving silhouettes, like vertical pen marks on a white page. The two in front are wheeling a small funeral cart, steam spreading from their nostrils and mouths and rising white into the grey sky. The corpses on the cart are laid neatly – only two this time, but one of them short, a child perhaps. The stomachs bloat beneath the blankets, forming small humps which the mantle of snow accentuates. The street is otherwise deserted. Hushed. Curlicued wrought-iron balconies lean silently out from the façades like crouching dark skeletons.

"It's almost beautiful," says Madame Pontellier quietly. Her breath mists against the cold glass.

"What's that you said?"

"Nothing, my darling," she murmurs as she slides sideways into her seat, one leg folded beneath her. She lifts her fork and spins it slowly between her fingers as she regards her casserole.

There is a knock on the door. They both look over to see Claudine enter. "Monsieur Courtois is here to see you, sir," she says.

As Pontellier rises the maid bobs her head and ducks out again. Courtois is hanging back in the dim hallway. "Come in," urges Pontellier.

"I've disturbed your lunch," says Courtois apologetically. "I should come back later," but he remains as he is, poised in the hallway.

"Nonsense." Pontellier gestures again for his friend to enter. "Please come in."

Awkward, Courtois hovers on the threshold, his eyes darting over the dinner table.

"Afternoon," says Madame Pontellier, still twisting her fork in her fingers. "Join us, if you wish, Monsieur Courtois, we've plenty," she says plainly, mistaking the preoccupation of his gaze for hunger.

"I'd rather not," he rushes. "Thank you all the same."

Recognising his friend's distress, Pontellier rises and touches Courtois's arm gently. "Would you prefer that we go downstairs?"

At Courtois's pained nod, he excuses them both and they leave Madame Pontellier in the room alone.

"Well, well, well," she says and stabs at a chunk of meat. After a few bites she lets her fork drop against the plate rim, spattering gravy onto the tablecloth, and stands up from the table.

It is just then, as she steps across the room, that her legs simply give way beneath her and Madame Pontellier collapses to the carpet. The shock of it winds her. She is utterly surprised, quite unsure at first if this could have been an action she had willed without realising it or whether something is actually wrong. She finds she is able to move her legs, but they feel clumsy, as if weights have been strung upon them. She doesn't get up. Waits instead to see if her fall has been heard by anyone.

She is close enough to smell the dusty wool of the carpet, to feel it prickle against her cheeks. Across the surface of its pattern, if she half-closes her eyes, it looks almost like a field of parched flowers, all pressed up against one another. She lets her eyes drift back across the surface of the carpet and again breathes in the sweetly arid smell of the wool.

Without purpose, she dips the tip of her tongue from her mouth and, very slowly, runs it over the rug.

No one has come to find her. She notes this suddenly and feels a bristle of annoyance. Raising herself, she twists her body round into a seated position. Her fingers lift to her mouth to pick at minuscule flecks of carpet fibre that have caught on her tongue. She wipes them afterwards on her dress front, then rearranges the pins in her hair. The maid should be called to clear the table, she thinks, heaving herself up to exit the room.

It is as she passes the stairwell that she hears the low murmur of their voices. She can't hear any words, just a sonorous lilt of distant sound. Only as she moves quietly down the wooden stairs does the sound begin to clarify, to break itself into distinct words and phrases. She doesn't even listen to the meaning, she is hearing only the rhythm and pattern of their speech, almost as though she were listening to a piece of music.

"I don't know what to do, Pontellier. I don't know how to pass the hours any more."

"Look, it can't last much longer."

"And when it does end, if it ever does? What then? What do I have left?"

"You can't think like that."

"How else can I think? I've lost everything. Good God, how could I have let this happen?"

"Quiet now...you *had* to do it, it wasn't a choice - people are starving in the streets."

"But I'm not helping *them*."

"You can't help them all."

His laugh is wry. "One evening last week, coming home, I passed one of those restaurants. The bright lights gaudy in the deserted street. A quartet playing a lively waltz that turned my soul, a very devil's dance it sounded to me. And there, at the glowing windows, I watched them in their finery. Laughing, joking, smacking lips glossy with grease. I turned away and retched onto the street." Neither man says anything for a moment. "That's who I'm 'helping', Pontellier. That's who. Society dames with their diamonds still looped round their necks, overweight lords chewing on their cigar ends, feyly poking at their dinner plates. And they, who have the privilege to dine on such 'delicacies', have the gall to jest – I've heard them – quipping that only the talent of our Parisian chefs could have made such 'quaint' dishes palatable - it makes me sick."

"Courtois."

"I reared those animals."

The soft murmur in response, words inaudible, fails to stop him from continuing. "That," he says clearly, his tone bitterly sardonic, "is how I am 'helping' to fight this war, Pontellier!"

"Look, you're helping *us*. Mireille. She wouldn't have survived without you, without your parcels."

"You're my only friend," he says simply, by way of explanation, then pauses as if defeated. "How is she faring?"

"Oh," he sighs, "so so. She's still a little…a little difficult at times but…it's nothing I'm not used to by now. I don't know, she barely acknowledges the world beyond her windowsill – comprehends nothing of the current situation. Nor does she, I believe, even care."

"Perhaps it's better that way. You don't want a recurrence."

"True."

"I should volunteer, shouldn't I? At least it would give me something to do."

"The same could be said for me, my friend. I've no business to speak of at present."

"It's really that bad?"

"Who has the money for a glass eye in times such as these?"

"I'm sorry."

"This siege can't last for ever. Something will have to give before too long."

In the hallway, while the two men have been speaking, Madame Pontellier has let the weight of her body slide slowly downwards against the wall. She is sitting now upon the floor, her legs pulled up before her. Her hands are clasped around her ankles. She can feel the cold of the tiles through her dress. The two men sitting at the desk in the shop space are out of her view. Their conversation barely distracts her, only the sound is what interests her, the shape of it in the dark hallway.

16th of December, 1870

IN THE SMALL hours of an austere December morning, the sky still dense with darkness, Pontellier is jolted from fretful dreams by the sound of screaming. His heart is launched instantly into a galloping frenzy which pounds heavy in his eardrums, vying with the noise that had awoken him. On opening, his eyes see nothing, too recently shielded by sleep are they. They stumble in their attempt to give shape to the sound.

It is the line of her shoulders, distinct beneath the white calico of her nightdress, that comes first into view. The curve of her back and shadowed periphery of her head appearing next, dreamily, like watching the pale torso of a swimmer surface in a dark pool.

He cannot see the black oval of her mouth, nor how it flattens itself each time she pauses to gulp in more breath, her body shuddering with the effort before relaxing itself again into the maintaining of the scream. Her whole consciousness is entirely focused upon the sound, obsessed by it. Its clarity is mesmerising; visible against the night. She can *see* the sound. It is like staring at a bright sun in the sky. That same dazzling funnelled intensity.

At the lace-like edges of the subconscious, her mind tousles with a recollection.

An autumn afternoon, standing in the high-walled garden of her childhood home. She cannot be more than five years old – a sturdy dark-haired child still in short skirts. She isn't alone, but with her parents and a number of others, though she's not quite sure who. They are assembled on the grass, chattering, exuding a nervous excitement. A voice above her says, "Listen, Mireille, even the birds have stopped their singing. You hear?" She nods, straining her ears to listen to the silence beyond them. The air is close as if waiting for a thunderstorm. "Help her with the spectacles so she can have a look," says another voice, and someone fumbles to catch the arms of a pair of wire-rimmed glasses about her ears. The lenses are so dark an indigo as to be almost black. The wire rests heavy on the bridge of her nose. "Up there, look at the sun," they say, guiding her gaze. And, where a moment before she remembered the bright haze of the sun, she now sees stencilled into the dark indigo sky of the spectacles a small white crescent moon. She grins at this curious trick. The moon is gone again as soon as they remove the glasses. Only if she squints at the brightness, then closes her eyes, can she see clearly the little crescent tattooed beneath her eyelids. "Careful," says someone, "if you stare too long at the sun it will leave you blind."

Too frightened to look upwards again, she keeps her

eyes downcast, staring at the grass, until that moment when, on that autumn afternoon of her childhood, the moon's shadow shifted fractionally in the sky above and the world slipped into darkness.

Jennifer Kabat

As If I Could Assume Your Life

This is a true story. It happened just after I moved to the country and I've held onto the facts of it, coddled them and kept them close, so I wouldn't forget, so one day I'd write it down. It was the day before Halloween and in that sense is a ghost story. It involves me and my neighbor, a woman named Dana Caruthers of whom I expected a fast, urgent friendship, the sort of which I was so fond. Indeed before I'd ever seen the inside of the house I was going to buy, I met her – over her picket fence. She held out her hand and said, "Dana, Dana Caruthers" and turned to tell two barking dogs to be quiet.

I told her I was Caitlin Skinner, introduced my husband Justin, and asked how long she'd lived here in Margaretville. I told her we didn't want to be in a village, that we were both decided on a place with twelve acres and outbuildings for Justin's studio.

"We bought land too," she said. "A farm out in Merridale but ended up renting it out. In the winter you want to be able to pop to the store for garlic or red wine, and just the idea of being there alone ..." She shuddered and the way she put it, needing a bottle of red wine sounded sophisticated. It was enough to convince me.

After we looked at the fussy Victorian with its turret and carriage house, we walked towards the realtor's car and Dana got up from her Adirondack chair. She dropped a magazine on the seat. She had a heart-shaped face, flushed skin and unruly russet-colored hair. Gardening gloves stuck out of the back pocket of her jeans. She looked to be 45, though later she'd admit to fifty. I was 35 that September and full of as much yearning as would fit in my five-foot-four frame. She said the owner of the house we'd seen had left to chair a department at Princeton.

"They can't keep three homes." She flipped over her palms as if to say, of course, doesn't everyone leave a rural village in upstate New York to teach at an Ivy League school? As if she knew I needed to hear there were smart people here doing career-minded things. It was true, I wanted to move to the country but worried no one would hire me to write magazine articles anymore if I left LA. Almost more than my worries about work, though were the fears of loneliness.

She asked if Justin was an artist and I said yes before he could. Anxious that she'd like me, I told her about his galleries in London and New York since he was too shy to tell strangers these things.

"And you?" Dana fixed her gaze on me. Her attention made me feel important.

"I'm a journalist – and then there's the fiction." I tried to laugh, looked down and noticed a rotten plank in the fence. When I glanced up, she was smiling. She brushed a strand of hair from her face.

"You know, I write too. We have so much to talk about clearly." She pressed her business card into my hand, and I never wondered about how quickly she'd found it as if she had been waiting for this. "You must, both of you must, come by my gallery and have a glass of wine."

THE REALTOR SHOWED us two more houses – a depressing farm that looked as if it were abandoned overnight and a ski chalet, that was yes, modern with lots of glass but totally wrong, too small. And I couldn't forget what Dana said about being lonely in winter.

ON THE DAY the sale went through, Justin was in LA at his fabricators' to see something for his show at the end of the month, so I went to the lawyer's alone. Justin sent flowers but still I felt an aching sadness expand in my ribs, and that night stood by myself in the new kitchen. The house echoed with silence except when the furnace shuddered on. I pulled out a drawer with stained contact paper and jumped when the phone rang. I was surprised to hear a woman's voice.

"We must do something to celebrate your closing." She sounded warm and melodious. "It's Dana," she said after a pause. I stood at the window, saw her across the street in her kitchen silhouetted against the light. We both waved.

I suggested a hike, told her I felt like I'd been trapped indoors. She said it would give us an excellent chance to talk, and I asked if ten miles was too much.

"Perfect," she said.

The clocks were changing that night, falling back for autumn and we agreed meeting at eight would allow plenty of time.

"We'll be done by two, three at the latest," I said just before hanging up.

The next morning I stood on her porch. It had two doors and I wasn't sure which she used, so knocked on what turned out to be the wrong one. When she answered I offered her a new trekking pole.

"I thought you could have the right and I'll take the left. We'll break them in."

She examined the pole, collapsed down to no more than a foot and emblazoned with florescent chevrons. She handed it back.

"We don't really need those. This is the Catskills, and it's not like our mountains are particularly high. Plus the snow's melted off anyway." Both of us looked at the scrubby hill in the distance, and I agreed it was silly but stuffed them in the orange backpack anyway.

The weather was supposed to be sixty-five, and indeed it was warm enough that I brought a hat but no gloves. Dana wore hand-knit mittens. We both assumed we didn't need anything more. There was a whole list of things we thought we wouldn't need like flashlight or matches and a list of assumptions about ourselves, that we were friends, that we were alike, that we could share things—feelings, work, anxiety.

On the way we stopped off at the Hess station to get Halloween candy. Dana wearily waved her hand in the air and said all the kids for miles around came trick or treating in the village, hundreds of them. But she always went out to dinner to avoid them. I wanted to be a good neighbor, though so bought four bags and the Sunday *New York Times*. She joked about bringing the magazine section to read while we ate lunch we'd have so much time.

She stopped by a sign for trailhead parking though the trail didn't start for a half mile more. We walked up a dirt road along a loud brook, past hunting cabins and weekenders' homes, a rickety bridge and storage shed, with its paint peeling and sign emblazoned "forestry service" – or at least that was what it looked like beneath the graffiti. A poster of "Winter Hiking Essentials" was nailed to a board. No jeans, no cotton, but pack extra food and clothing.

I laughed and said, "It's a good thing we're not hiking in winter then."

"Feels like spring, doesn't it?"

When we reached the trailhead sign-in, the last date in the log was more than a month before.

"Guess we'll have it all to ourselves," Dana said as she put down our names and route. Not even ten yards away, though, close enough that he no doubt heard us, a hunter leaned against a tree and smoked. A starkly futuristic bow was propped next to him. Its elegant arcing form made me think of bones.

When he heard where we were going, he said, "I couldn't do that," and shook his head. All of him was lean, wiry but for a belly, which he patted for emphasis. "Not no more I couldn't. That's a long hike there, ladies, but I've never been far on the trail, here. You don't stick to the trails with deer."

I said bow hunting had to be hard, that there had to be an art to it. He agreed and talked about a one-ness he got with the deer, a feeling, he called it, and it sounded almost Buddhist – except for his killing them.

He stamped out his cigarette and we wished each other luck.

A DISCREET DISTANCE away I said he seemed nice. I was always apt to like people from the start, it was only after

I got to know them that my opinion changed, and Justin would listen to me say, oh god, I can't believe it, did you see what so and so did?

Dana shook her head. "But hunting? It's just horrid. All they want to exercise is their blood lust. If they can't go to war and kill a man, they figure they might as well take a deer."

"But how do you know he's like that?"

"Because I used to love a hunter once. They're all alike." She sniffed, and as if to keep me from asking more said, "In December you'll see. There'll be carcasses strapped to cars, gun racks, the whole nine. Well, Justin'll be horrified." Dana knew he was a vegetarian, but I liked venison and didn't really think there was much wrong with hunting. I changed topics. We were still trying to be friends.

We both laughed when we came on the first patches of snow on the trail. I jumped into a pile of it for effect. Dana threw snowballs at a tree, and I asked why she'd moved to the sticks.

She told me about Ohio about going when her husband Toby got a tenure track job. "I had to give up on my own PhD – for Columbus, of all places." She'd planned on finishing her degree in Ann Arbor and driving between the two. "But it felt like too much. The first time I tried to go, it was snowing, and I just couldn't do it."

I told her I understood, but wondered how she could give up on something that mattered so much to her because of some bad weather.

THE SNOW WAS so heavy as we walked, the weight of it had saplings bent double. I shook the first one and announced they needed saving. We both ran and brushed the snow off the trees, flinging it in the air and down our shirts. Dana laughed and neither of us thought about the sign, the winter hiking essentials, and how we weren't supposed to wear cotton. Instead we tried to keep track of the trees we saved, and that slowed us down more, that and the snow getting deeper the higher we climbed. She didn't say anything about how there were always early wet snows and still the trees survived, that we just weren't there to see.

"You know," Dana jerked a tree in her hand, "Toby, just wouldn't do this, all he wants when he's back is to sleep – or read, and it's like I have this weekend husband commuting from a teaching gig in New York. Of course he's at a conference in Montreal now." She held out her hands in mock surrender. It seemed as if she'd been waiting for this moment to confide in me – as if she was as desperate for companionship as I – only she needed to talk about her husband and me my writing. But I didn't. I felt the words well up, I could imagine them in my head, how I'd start by saying that I really wanted a reader. Instead I found myself nodding when she said, "Of course when he comes home the house is always clean. With six animals it's a daily job. And could he be grateful? No."

I murmured, yeah, of course, though I wasn't sure I agreed, I didn't even really know Toby. He was a poet, taught college in Brooklyn now. "Thirteenth grade," he'd said the one time we'd met. I was at the house for the inspection and he joked about his remedial English class in the state system.

"His whole idea of cooking is ordering Chinese." She kicked at the snow in front of her.

I wanted to join in and say... what? Tell her I was jealous of Justin's success? Or that I hated how shy he was? Instead I offered up my parents.

"My mom thinks my dad can't do anything either, but she never even gives him a chance to fail. My shrink says she complains because she just needs someone to listen." Dana looked down and pulled off a mitten.

"Isn't it a glorious day?" she said, and I wondered if she was changing the subject.

AT THE TOP of the ridge there were no footprints in the slush in either direction. Deer tracks crossed the trail in places, some prints that looked like dog too but had to be coyote, and as we continued on the path, there were bear markings. I wondered how long they'd been there and assumed they were fresh. If they'd been old, the outlines would have melted into a blur.

Dana didn't notice or if she did, didn't say anything. She walked quietly along the ridgeline with views through the trees, and the sky was so blue, it was as if we could see the outer atmosphere. I was still waiting for a moment to mention my writing, but I couldn't break the silence not till she suggested lunch. I brushed the snow off a boulder and spread on top the two A&P bags that had held our sandwiches. As we ate I stared in the distance at the mountains and a farm hidden in a valley. The sun looked to be dropping already. I asked which way was west.

Dana shrugged and said she wasn't sure. From where I sat, slightly above her on the rock I noticed the gray roots of her hair. She pointed in the opposite direction.

"It's that way. You can't see the reservoir, and that's west of us. Definitely." It was a relief, but neither of us wore a watch or realized it had gone two already. Our assumptions about time were all wrong because of the clocks' changing. I thought it was noon at the latest, though I couldn't be this hungry so early. I didn't say anything though, just offered Dana some M&Ms.

"I don't do sugar, just wine." She waved like a bored starlet and I told her I had to take a picture of her, just like that. In the shot it looked like she was smiling though it was hard to tell. She was dark against the bright blue sky.

When we started again, Dana said her shirt was still wet, her legs cold and her calves cramping. The water had wicked up the denim and darkened her jeans almost to the knees. Instead of offering to turn around, I suggested looking at the map. I held it out for us to examine together. Later, I'd remember the way the map felt in my hands, the paper soft like fabric even though it was waterproof, and I'd regret not turning back, just as in another light I'd have heard what the hunter said as a warning.

On the way down from the ridge Dana told me how she got to Margaretville. She didn't mention the affair she'd had with a professor, a writer in Columbus. Instead I'd piece that together during the hike, and she talked about the string of homes behind her, her place in Ohio, a miserable apartment back in Brooklyn, where she'd felt isolated after September 11 and announced to Toby that they had to leave the city. They'd moved first to Kingston and that being lonely too, soon to Margaretville. While her loneliness matched mine, I also judged it and thought about all those houses, calculated that it couldn't have been more than two years in each. I watched her mouth, the lines along it as she described the pool in Ohio, the snake she'd found in it once and wondered what she was running from. I decided to talk to her about my writing. That was really the reason I moved, wasn't it? If I was honest with myself.

The words came out so full of longing I didn't even sound normal. I told her how excited I was she was my neighbor. How much I wanted a friend, someone to share work with, someone struggling too. But I couldn't know that Dana didn't want to hear this. She'd told Toby she'd write in the country, that all she'd needed was the time and space. Only she'd found herself pacing the house and unable to focus, so she took the job at the gallery and didn't want to get involved with my creative struggles.

"I just can't engage anymore with that kind of pain. The whole thing of trying to write, hoping to be… Very adolescent," she said.

I focused on the ground, at the rocks we had to climb down and the soggy leaves trapped in the crevices. A loose stone echoed as it fell. The sound reverberated with my own anxiety, and I got out a pole so I wouldn't lose my balance on the steep path.

From the bottom I watched Dana descend. She was hunched over, to keep her center of gravity low. Her hands and face were clenched in concentration. I wanted to talk about Justin, his collectors and dealers, and the waiting list for his work as if his success would protect me. Only before I could, she stumbled.

Her arms cartwheeled out from her, her right hand flung towards a boulder to break her fall. Her mouth was open, as if about to yell as I ran towards her. I helped her up and when she was standing, asked if she was okay, if she wanted a pole. She brushed her hands together no doubt to get the ice off, but the gesture seemed designed to dismiss me.

"I'm sure I'm faster without that thing." She took it anyway.

I extended it and said if it weren't the right height I'd fix it.

"How would I know the right height?" She stabbed at some moss with the sharp tip.

THE TRAIL PLUNGED until it reached Ploutz Road, a dirt track that dead-ended in the woods. The air smelled sweet of rotting leaves and pine needles and the ground was wet.

I suggested trying to hitchhike and said, "I'm sure if we walk down the road, we'll get a ride." Dana didn't respond and I asked if her hip still hurt.

"It's fine. We have to be near the end." A small muscle in her cheek throbbed, and I pretended not to hear her say under her breath how she'd wished we'd turned back before lunch – or after the hunter.

"Yeah, and who knows how long it'll take us to find a car?" My voice curled up and Dana looked down as if she was studying the Christmas fern that remained green despite the cold. She turned to me and smiled.

"You know, I taught writing in Columbus at Ohio State, creative writing and intro comp, and this girl, a junior wrote about me. In her story I was having an affair with someone else in the department, Jack, Jack Tilton." She paused while I registered the name. He'd been nominated for a few book awards a decade ago.

"He was teaching there, so she had us having an affair. Oh we'd ride around in his pickup and meet secretly at his place, she said. As if she could know, as if she could assume my life. So I called her into my office and said, 'Look around, you've never been to office hours, never taken a step in here the entire semester. You got the details all wrong, honey. Now don't you go and try to steal my life again." Dana looked at me as if I and the girl, or at least my image of her in a baggy OSU sweatshirt and tight jeans, were one and the same.

"You see, I don't take well to people appropriating my territory." She seemed to study my face, and it was clear she meant this as a warning even if she didn't recognize it as such. In that moment though I could see the story I needed to write – not about Dana and this man or her student but about the two of us. She'd be jealous and disillusioned by me, her new neighbor who was so similar it was ghostly. We'd both be involved in art and writing. Yes, I could see it. I'd write it from her point of view, only I had no idea how the next two hours would create the necessary drama.

The sun was just above the brow of the hill, and silver light raked over the trunks of trees as we climbed up. It would disappear soon. At the top it would be okay, but the sun was setting, and there was no question now which way was west. Dana seemed untroubled though, glancing down as if absorbed in her own thoughts.

"Dana, it's getting late. We've got to get out of here. We need to run."

"Stop being so dramatic." She shook her head with disgust and plucked a twig from her mitten.

I marched ahead and looked back, wondered what I ever saw in this woman dawdling as she stopped to adjust her pole. It was as if she was going slowly just to make a point. As we started down the hill, the light faded. The color drained from everything.

"Look, were not even near the end, the path has a steep descent where it zigzags down. We need to try and make it out."

"Okay, okay, whatever you say." Despite her exasperated tone, she looked relieved.

We both ran. She had on boots like sneakers with no ankle protection but a beefed up sole, and the path was rocky. I knew if she fell, she could twist her ankle, maybe even break it. Still we sprinted, panting, and my backpack chafed against my lower back. Dana slowed and I told her to hurry up.

"But we need to make a shelter, a bivvy or whatever they call it. We need a plan." Her words were breathless and choppy.

"Yeah, to get out of here. We need to keep going."

In the last moments of waning light she stopped and stood there. Said she couldn't see the markers anymore. She closed her eyes for a dramatically long time and rubbed her brow. "You can't kill me, I cannot die out here. My death will be on your hands. And I just wanted to do something nice. Brunch would have suited me fine."

I didn't respond, just said quietly, "Do you think the hunter will check the registration log, to see if we signed out?" I didn't think she'd heard.

"He won't even consider it – all he wants is his kill. And to think you liked him. That should have clued me in. I should have turned around right there and then. My loss, I guess." She laughed for a second and sobbed. "I am going to die here in the cold and wind. Alone."

I could barely make out the trail markers. They were no longer red, just gray in the twilight, but if I squinted I could see them. It was too dark to run, so we walked slowly till one came into view. I wondered about Justin. I was cold, wearing two damp t-shirts and a fleece. I tried to walk with my hands in my pockets, but that only made me less stable. How long would it take him to realize I was lost? I remembered the day we got married at a friend's house in Los Feliz by the pool. At the party after in Chinatown, I'd worn a red dress and purple patent-leather heels. My mother got drunk and upbraided my father for his toast.

Soon it was too dark to see the markers or path no matter how much I squinted. Dana panicked and I walked ahead feeling each tree for the two-inch disk that would say we were going the right way. When I found one, I'd talk Dana to where I stood, guiding her with my voice and I'd leave her clinging to the tree while I tried to find the next. It wasn't long until there was no next one though. I'd walked what – twenty, thirty feet, I couldn't even judge the distance anymore. I groped each tree. I thought about how soft the moss was on one and how I'd heard as a kid about the Underground Railroad, that the moss grew on the north side of trees and slaves used it to guide them. I wondered if it worked, if we could navigate that way.

We had a quarter bottle of water left, four, maybe six

ounces. And one packet of M&Ms I'd taken from the bags of Halloween candy. I was hungry. Dana must have been too, but I knew I had to save them. If we were still here at six am, we'd need the sugar then.

I crossed a small stream and suggested following it down. Had it not snowed that week the creek would have been dry and even now it was barely a trickle. "It has to join that brook we cross to reach the road," I said, only Dana protested, insisted there was a reason the path had switchbacks.

"Who knows what's down there, rocks or boulders? If it were passable it would go straight. ... Oh god," she said after a long pause. She clutched her stomach and coughed. I could just make out her hunched form as she retched a few feet away. There was no moon that night, only ambient light from the stars.

I offered her the water, and she said she'd get some from the stream instead. Her voice was imperious, haughty even after throwing up, haughty in the face of all this. She wiped her mouth on her sleeve when she stood up and demanded my camera.

"We can use it to see the map, and maybe the trail." I had to agree it was a good idea.

She held the map and I took the pictures. I wondered if she too found the paper soft, surprising, but didn't ask, just said, "Look I'll go first, I'll lead. It'll be fine."

"Fine? You're going to take us off the trail into god-knows-what, and you're saying it's fine?"

I couldn't admit how frightened I was, just said, "Give me your hand."

She did too, didn't put up any more struggle, even gave me a mitten to wear. I wondered if that little gesture of intimacy could make up for everything else. Her skin felt dry like paper against my fingers, and her bones were so fine they made me think of a tiny animal – and the arcing curve of the hunter's bow. I could feel her knuckles and wondered about the joints. I didn't remember what her hands looked like, but thought of the base communion in trying to save our lives, walking in the dark, lost, terrified. My mouth tasted of fear.

I speared the ground in front of me with the pole and described each thing I found, the stumps, roots and rocks. "There's a stone here and a tree down and another just past that. To your right's a rock. Don't step on it, it's loose." Repeating each detail was calming. My voice was level as if clawing our way down the side of a mountain was normal.

The strategy was fine for the deciduous trees, which had lost their leaves. The thin starlight let me see a foot or so in front of me, but when we came to the stands of pines, even the stars were blotted out, and the low boughs, the bare branches at the base of the trees, scratched my face and neck. I held Dana's hand tighter, my heart raced and I wondered if we'd survive. A pile of rocks I hadn't noticed slid out from under me, and I nearly fell, but caught my weight on the pole. My throat hurt with the tension and the cold air burned my nostrils. I wondered how long it would take someone to find my body here and remembered that freezing to death was supposed to be peaceful, like going to sleep. I was so scared I wanted to die right there.

"It's below freezing. We need to make a plan." Dana yelled about shelter and help and her husband. I told her to be quiet and apologized quickly.

"What about the animals – coyotes, bears? What about them? I've heard coyotes hunt deer now, in packs with a pincer action around them. I just think –" She stopped as if trying to consider what she thought. "I need to sit a second."

I was relieved. I'd wanted to sit but was too scared to

suggest it. She settled on a damp tree trunk and sobbed, no tears, just violent dry huffs.

"Jack was a hunter."

I realized what she was saying, the small admission in her words, and reached for her shoulder.

"Don't fucking touch me!"

"Okay, okay."

"He was so tough. He smoked and drank whiskey – and was a total shit. I loved him."

I nodded though she couldn't see me. I felt sad and sorry and thought I knew why she'd left Ohio and ranted about the hunter earlier. I wanted to tell her I understood, and when she stood up again, I took back her hand. She didn't fight me. I remembered when I'd met Toby he was driving a pickup. I could picture Dana insisting he get it as if it could bring her closer to Jack. I wondered if Toby knew and described the branches at my feet. Dana interrupted me.

"Water, can you hear it? It's the brook. We're getting closer." We both stood still and listened. It sounded like a fan or an engine from where we were. When we reached the edge, I asked if we should walk upstream to find the bridge.

"Yeah, we've come this far to fall on an outcropping of rocks?" Sarcasm cut through each word.

"What do you think we should do then?" I turned to her but no doubt she couldn't see my disgust. My sympathy for her was gone.

"I don't know, how am I supposed to know? You brought me here."

I slapped her. "Can you just shut up?" She didn't say anything just held her hand to her cheek where I'd hit her.

"Well, I'm crossing. You can stand there and make your own decisions."

I squatted down at the edge, on a rock that seesawed under my weight. I got out the camera to take a picture so I could see how deep the water was. The flash lit the streambed and the first shot reflected off the bottom but gave no sense of depth, the next captured the white water on top, and the third was only a smoky blur.

"Let me try." She ripped away the camera.

It fell in the water and I just looked at her. "I don't believe you. Fuck it, I'm going across."

"Wait, I'm coming too."

The water was shockingly cold, it seeped over the top of my boots, all the way up to my knees. The current was stronger than I'd expected, and I slid on a rock but hauled myself out. I didn't consider the danger, not until I was on the other side. If I'd realized, maybe I'd have stayed there all night.

"Just grab onto my pole," I said and thought about letting her fall in. I didn't tell her if she did, there was no way to see her or save her. Her arms flailed above her head, and as I hoisted her out, headlights appeared on the road above.

She scrambled onto the bank and up to the road. She waved her one pole in the air, but the red taillights glowed in the dark as the truck drove past. Just beyond us, illuminated in the headlights, was the bridge. I laughed at what was lost, what might have been, and my wet feet squished in the waterlogged boots. We walked in silence maybe a half-mile more looking for her car. Inside, I apologized for hitting her. I handed her a bag of Halloween candy. She stared at it, sniffed in disgust and turned on the ignition.

OVER THE NEXT few months Dana turned into a specter of herself. She gained weight and let her hair go gray with a line halfway down her head where her natural color met the fading red dye as if that marked the moment of her change. I started to assume her friends and heard she got fired from the gallery. A week later there was an ad in the local paper for her replacement. Someone suggested I apply, said it'd be a good way to meet people, but I couldn't do it.

I'd told myself her deterioration wasn't my fault and wrapped myself tight in self justification, only I kept returning to the moment when I'd slapped her and she'd confessed about Jack. I wanted to change those things, to take them back. Instead I moved my office to the other side of the house so I wouldn't have to see her, but at night when I stood in the kitchen I'd see her turn on a light and watch her silhouetted in the window and could feel her haunting me. It got worse a few months later when I stopped seeing the lights at all.

I ran into Toby one Sunday at the A&P. "How are you. And – how's Dana? Tell her I asked about her," I said, but he was already gone, pushing his cart up the aisle with its stained linoleum floors.

A few days later I went to apologize. I couldn't take it any longer. I took some flowers from my garden, tulips and daffodils that were in bloom, and knocked at her door. No one answered. I left the bouquet there on the porch and watched over the next week as the petals fell off the tulips and the daffodils shriveled and turned brown.

MECCA JAMILAH SULLIVAN

Adale

THE STINK OF burnt oatmeal seemed to hang from the brownstone kitchen's cherrywood beams, perpetually in idle swing like the stray pairs of sneakers that used to hang from the Harlem streetlamps outside. Dominique Potter had burnt fourteen pots of oatmeal among the half-packed boxes by the second Sunday of 2005. Weeks before, she had been known to burn only the outermost oats of a given pot, and those only so slightly that most of the soft mush within could be plied with butter or crusted with brown sugar and salvaged after all. Now, her son Mandela had to wait at the table for an hour each morning while his mother turned on the oven and opened its door for heat, poured the first pot, stirred it, turned to the news, got lost in the tsunami and let the oats burn. Eventually, she would return to the stove barely more vigilant, yet keeping the wooden spoon in her hand this time to assure the safety of all or most of the second pot of the day. Dominique had spent much of her time in that kitchen since the day after Christmas, packing boxes and cooking meals, standing before that stove, her spine arced back and her stomach bounding out before her, holding the ragged spoon in one hand and her stomach in the other, watching a whirl of shattered dark- and light-gray faces on television, and thinking of the wet honey-colored face that would sprout from between her legs in only weeks.

Images of ruin lit the television screen those mornings. Pictures of broken bodies, of houses and towns halved and quartered as though bit into by great celestial fangs hung beside the heads of reporters with perfectly cropped hair and baffled eyes. It seemed to Dominique, during the first few days, that each hour the number on which their voices hung trembling climbed to digits she could scarcely imagine. *What would one hundred thousand of something look like*, she had thought that Wednesday, contorting her tongue around the t-and-s-heavy word that splashed from the reporters' mouths like water kicked up from a puddle. *What would one hundred thousand be?* She tried to imagine the one hundred thousand stars they might find at night in the Poconos, where the family would be moving in two weeks. Stroking the baby girl, Adale, who pressed against the lining of her stomach, she tried to imagine what even one hundred thousand blades of grass would look like be when they arrived. Her mind crawled and clawed at these images as she leaned into the small black-and-white television, planting herself among the torn trees, searching the screen for a way to understand. Eventually, Mandela would call her back from the ripped beaches and tell her, coughing and sneezing, that their breakfast had begun to burn.

THE BOY WAS very patient those mornings. He emerged from their bedroom shortly after Dominique woke up, climbed down the creaking brownstone stairs behind her, and stationed himself at the edge of the long wooden table, his arms stretched across the one-and-a-half square feet of striped wood that was not covered with flat cardboard boxes, his grandmother's trinkets or his grandfather's mail. He coughed and sneezed quietly as Dominique tended to the stove, his feet stretched across the floor beneath the table, and watched the television blink and speed in reels off the top of the screen, only to return from the bottom, mere nanoseconds of action having passed. Mandela did not let show his disappointment with the news clips (which seemed to him to have been exactly the same each morning since Christmas, yet which were repeated incessantly, for some reason he could not understand, and which had even barged in and interrupted his cartoons once or twice this week). He was grateful for his cold and his extended Christmas vacation, happy to spend his mornings coughing here in the air-bitten kitchen among blinking pictures and the smell of burnt grains and oven heat, instead of at school.

MRS. POTTER, DOMINIQUE's mother, had applauded her grandson's patience a number of times over this vacation, particularly on Christmas morning, when he awoke around 5 AM, roused, she was sure, by the excitement that seemed to run like bugs over children's skin on that one day each year. She had heard him creak from the bedroom he and her daughter shared and had heard his socked feet scamper over the linoleum-covered stairs to the family room to find the spread she was sure would disappoint him: a cheap plastic backpack, two paper-back books about rainforest turtles, and three dubbed and hand-marked CDs, all wrapped in last year's paper and arrayed sparsely beneath the tree.

In all the years past, since Dominique was a child, Mrs.

Potter had seen to it that their tree sprawled gifts like the trees on the sets of her favorite heart-warming holiday shows and movies. Late Christmas eve, once the child (Dominique until her 16th birthday, then Mandela the year after) had gone to sleep, Mr. Potter would lay or squat on the living room floor beside the tree, his tools spread around him as he assembled the dream house, the five-part stereo or whatever thing would serve as the center-piece gift that year. Returning from midnight Mass, Mrs. Potter would then drag all of the smaller gifts she had bought the child over the past year from shopping bags wedged in the bottom of her closet and station herself at the dinging room table among rolls of tape and reams of shiny wrapping paper, cutting little rectangles of paper with which to label each gift. Some she would sign from her husband and herself ("Mom and Dad" first, then "Grandma and Pop-Pop"), some from Santa (these marked with notes like "Ho, Ho, Ho, thanks for the cookies!,") and, for the past seven years, some *from Dominique* ("Love, Mama").

It became clear early enough on that two thousand four's Christmas spread would not be so resplendent, as Mr. Potter had lost his management job at the Port Authority the previous December and was now only days away from seeing his unemployment run out. Dominique's job at the new Pathmark on 145th street enabled her to buy her own clothes and, most importantly, groceries for the family, but nothing more. Mrs. Potter's monthly struggles to balance the mortgage, the utilities, and the provision of clothing for herself, her husband, and her grandchild had failed on more than one occasion, so that in November she had had to establish the family's new habit of opening the oven door to warm the kitchen of the rickety brownstone to save on heat. Mrs. Potter did what she could with her medical assistant's salary for two thousand four's gifts, wrapping each item – each book, each CD – individually, so that she was able to spread six gifts beneath the small plastic shrub she had bought on sale at a flea market last summer and call it Christmas. She had marked the drably-colored foam-stuffed backpack from her and Mr. Potter (who had closed himself off in the living room since the anniversary of his unemployment, leaving her to assemble the meager Christmas spread alone). The CDs she labelled *from Santa* with a cheery note, and the turtle books from Dominique. She awoke Christmas morning prepared to fold the child into her breasts and assure him as best she could that things would be better once they had moved. When she pushed through the living room door, however, she found the skinny boy perched cross-legged on the old brown sofa, a book in his lap, the latest urban radio station compilation album playing low on the stereo.

"Grandma," he had said, his mouth gaping wide, displaying his missing front tooth. He tilted his sleep-crusted eyes up at her. "Did you know that snapping turtles can't snatch their heads up under their shells like the other kinds?"

Mrs. Potter had shaken her head and invited the boy to come with her to the kitchen where she could start dinner while he helped pack the good dishes and told her more about it. She hoped that this next grandchild would be so patient, as she was not entirely sure that even two or three years of the low rent and no-tax living in the Poconos (less than half of their mortgage) would repair the family's situation. She hoped her granddaughter would somehow take more after her brother than Dominique, that she would share Mandela's maturity, his perspective and sensibility not unlike Mrs. Potter's own. It had been Mandela, after all, who silenced his disconsolate twenty-three year-old mother when Mrs. Potter informed the family that they would be losing the house.

"Now that things are getting nice around here, of course we have to leave," the girl had shrieked, bouncing to her feet and pushing the dining room table away from her as though it had provoked her to fight. "As soon as some good stores show up and the place starts looking better. Now that people are starting to notice us, now we have to go." She had turned to Mrs. Potter then, her eyes sharp as box cutter blades. "And what about Adale? You want her to grow up out in the sticks in an apartment so cheap the building advertises on TV? No black people around, no stores, no music. No streets! Or did you forget about her?"

Mrs. Potter had not responded to her daughter's tantrum, except by passing thoughts over the inner rim of her lips and sucking her teeth as she cleared the table. Mr. Potter, too, had stayed silent, filling his glass with water and lifting it to his face to crunch on the ice. Mandela had spoken, though, quietly from his chair at the foot of the table.

"Maybe she'll like the country, Mama."

DOMINIQUE ALLOWED HER friends to believe that she had named Mandela for his father, a corner crack slinger named Nelson. It was a convenient explanation – her friends thought it was a smart way to make the boy a junior without giving him a corny name. They liked the way it sounded, too, although Rashida and Yunnique said it might be too effeminate and thought he might have to make up for it in wildness or extreme intelligence to avoid being beaten up. Really, though, Dominique was not concerned with her baby's father, nor was she worried that anyone would threaten her son. She named Mandela for the real Nelson, but more for a vague period of time that represented, in her mind, the best qualities a young man could have – strength, wisdom, loud power and patience in struggle. She named him for the time of Public Enemy videos and black fist air bush tees which, when Dominique had first begun to dream of babies, seemed to her to be a permanent black mark history's timeline. At sixteen, she had thought only that her son, like the era of red, yellow and green in which she grew up, would be respected, formidable, difficult for the world to deny and impossible for it to forget. She did not mention to anyone her profound disappointment when she noticed the colors of that time beginning to fade. When the African street vendors on 125th street were swept from the sidewalk and piled into a dirty tent on Lenox Avenue, she only sighed with Yunnique and shook her head. When the H.M.V. music store and the Modell's Sporting Goods cropped up shiny and sleek in the vendors' place and her girls got ready to shop, eager to buy real CDs in their own neighborhood, Dominique went along, folding the tables of bootleg tapes that had once lined the street into her memory.

She may have gone wrong with Mandela's name, but she would be sure with Adale. Adale was not, Dominique knew, the name of a man whose life could evaporate into history's stale air once the drama of his struggle subsided. Nor was it inspired by a time, which, she now knew, could be buried under the new and forgotten. It was not a name any of her friends had heard of, though they all agreed it was cute. Dominique had discovered her daughter's name early one morning shortly after Mandela was born. He had woken the entire house crying, and once she and her mother had quieted him and put him down again, Dominique had been unable to sleep. There had been little to watch on television, and so she found herself watching a bushy-haired white man on a charity infomercial as he slogged through moats of brown skin and garbage, the camera zooming in now and then on a pair of milk-pool eyes or a row of porcelain teeth. Speaking earnestly, a frail brown child dangling over his shoulder, the man urged the camera to send money to one of these children, the beautiful, starving children of Adale, Somalia.

Dominique had known nothing about Africa, except that it was the smallest unit of place to which her blood could ultimately be traced, and that it was not small enough for that fact to mean much, especially now that that vague Africa for which she had named her son had become so scarce on the streets of Harlem. Still, she remembered Somalia. She remembered hearing the name of that place from all directions not long before. She remembered seeing its name on the front covers of newspapers and hearing it come through the mouth of her white junior high school math teacher with more emotion than she had thought white math teachers able to muster. To see, then, years later that this place was still important, still calling the world's attention in the dusty hours of the morning, had struck Dominique softly in her stomach. She hadn't felt she could send any money, having just had a baby for a useless man, having left school for the baby and not yet having found a job. Still, she took note. The paper on which she wrote the name in her round bubble lettering was lost within a year, but neither the name nor its spelling had escaped her.

BY THE SECOND Sunday of the year, the number on the screen had climbed to 156,000. An anchorwoman with swirling golden-brown hair sat straight and stiff at her desk as a house was swept in white foam in the box over her shoulder. Her elbows flapped at her sides as she read the number in a low, unsteady voice, the s-word lunging from her lips again.

"Mama, that's how a snapper looks," Mandela said, looking up at Dominique from the table, one of Mrs. Potter's pharmaceutical logo pens in his hand. "Like that lady." He pressed the button on the back of the pen, tapping his feet against a box on the floor along with the clicking sound.

"Ssh, Mandela, I'm trying to listen," she said quickly. Then, looking at her son, she added: "Go wash your hands. I'ma start breakfast."

Standing between cardboard boxes in the near-empty

pantry, she opened the glass canister where the rice had been kept and tried to imagine one hundred fifty six thousand grains. The ten pound bag of oatmeal she had bought from work for only five dollars, (with coupon savings and her employee discount) had lasted almost a month, and would have lasted twice as long, she reminded herself, had the news not so distracted her from feeding her son. But now only powder and scattered oats remained at the bottom of the limp plastic bag. She called up the stairs after Mandela, telling him that she was going to the store, and to listen to Pop-Pop and finish packing his room while she was gone, as he would have to go back to school tomorrow. Leaving the television on, Dominique pulled her yellow bubble jacket from the hall closet and wrapped her peach scarf around her neck, preparing to trudge through the gray air and cold concrete to the supermarket on her day off.

The white couple who had bought the brownstone next door and who, Mrs. Potter had told her, were likely to soon come up with the down payment on their own house and convert it into high-rent floor-throughs, had laid a huge evergreen lazily across the seam of the pavement. Dominique lifted her leg high to step over its trunk, clearing the sidewalk that still belonged, she remarked, to her family. She rounded the corner and proceeded down Broadway. The wide avenue unfolded slowly under a heavy pall of fog. The movement this Sunday was sparse and slow, perhaps, Dominique imagined, because most people were warm at home watching the news. A bare-legged blonde woman in a short skirt and knee-high boots walked toward her, holding limply in her left hand a pair of black sunglasses that looked like the Diors Dominique had admired in the tabloid magazines that gilded her aisle at work. The woman stomped the row of concrete slabs beside Dominique as though by the force of her gait and the swift jaunting of her pink knees she was able not simply to move forward, as Dominique and most people she knew did, but rather to push the streets aggressively behind her with the backs of her thick black heels.

Reaching within a few feet of Dominique, the woman turned her head and gave an open-mouthed half-smile. Dominique had seen this expression regularly on these new faces over the past few years, but she had never quite been able to read it. Dominique parted her lips in response and felt only cool air in the sides of her mouth as the woman's body cut the breeze in swift passing. Cold pricking against her teeth, Dominique thought of Adale, how the wind in her face would be different; cooler than this gust stirred up in the blonde woman's wake, cleaner, Dominique imagined, with the taste of pine or mint. Her baby girl would be born into a grove of tall dark trees whose bushy green tops would crowd the sky and spread out only on the wind's urging, and then only slightly, only to allow blots and shafts of sun to pass through. The sun would pass gently, she imagined. It would thank the ushering branches and slide thick as honey toward the soft brown ground, where there would be mud, grass, she and her family out there, somewhere, in a short two-bedroom house, but with heat, the rent paid, more and better food to eat. It would not be so bad, she insisted to herself.

Scattered clusters of church women inched from the narrow blocks to Broadway's curbs in low, clinking heels, past the police barricades and heaps of renovation lumber that lined some of the corners, piling into sleek town cars for the six or seven dollar ride to Sunday service. Dominique recognized some of these women and gave them a pleasant smile as she passed. One woman rolled down the back window of a maroon Lincoln and stuck her hand out into the air, shaking her fingers in an enthusiastic flutter to halt Dominique in front of the G.N.C.

"Hey, baby!" Her brown lips emerged in relief from the black cavern of the cab.

"Hi." Dominique smiled warmly, only half-attempting to remember the name of this woman who had surely known but had not needed to remember hers. "How you doin' this mornin'?"

"Fine, baby, don't pay to complain." The car bobbed as someone in the back seat rustled in impatience. The woman smiled and pointed to Dominique's stomach. "When you due?"

"Five weeks." A smile spread across Dominique's face and stung her cheeks and forehead with heat. "Hopefully she' be a Valentine's baby."

"Well God bless you!" The cab began to roll forward. "Tell your mother I said happy New Year! Tell her make sure she call me fore y'all go. My sister's out there, Ella, you remember. She'll show y'all around." The voice trailed off as the window screeched up into its groove and the car fled ahead. A white man in sweat pants bowled through the door of the G.N.C., pushing a wave of heat at Dominique's face as he walked past her, the little brown dog that trailed behind him stepping on her feet. She felt Adale kick.

She turned the corner on 145th, where a group of people had gathered in front of the scaffolded building where, it had been said, a new Radio Shack was being built. Slender, young-looking figures in baseball caps and scarves unfolded tables and hauled cardboard boxes out of an open van parked on the corner. Dominique passed the scene and continued down the hill she had walked every morning for the past three months, since the Pathmark opened, and down which she would walk for only two weeks more.

Entering the Pathmark, Dominique said hello to the bag check man and a few of the stockers. She made a lap around the crowded market's periphery, as she did whenever she came here on her days off, glad to have the time to survey all the cheeses she had never tasted, the different types of yogurt and milk, the packs of dips and sauces chilling

coolly on their shelves. Weaving in and out of carts pushed
by gloved and pea-coated students and big brown women
in dress coats in the bakery corner, Dominique admired
the fancy strawberry- and date-filled pastries which, she
remembered excitedly, would be on sale in a week. Her
back began to ache a little as she passed the walls of produce
where yellows and oranges and greens bolder than any color
she had seen on food before surprised her every time she
glanced in that direction of the supermarket. She waved to
a few of the other cashiers and said hello to the Dominican
boy who arranged the displays in the butcher section as
she rounded the corner of the cereal aisle. Stooping before
the wholesale-size bags and boxes on the bottom shelf, she
discovered that the ten-pound oatmeal was no longer on
sale. She counted the days until they would leave New
York, multiplied by two, and slid a four pound cardboard
canister off of the middle shelf instead.

"Beautiful," the only male cashier, a young cherry-
colored African man, said, smiling at her from the register
of the aisle next to hers. "What are you doing here on
Sunday?"

"I gotta make breakfast." Dominique shrugged and
smiled limply, sitting the canister on the shiny black
conveyer belt. His accent reminded her of the way 125th
street used to sound, its vowels stuffed with cotton and its
consonants both sharp and blunt like old nails. She waited
for him to talk some more.

"When will it be time for baby number two?" He
passed the oatmeal over the scanner and continued without
pausing. "That one will be another boy. He sits low."

"No." Dominique shook her head softly, looking at
the tall white figures in limp, slack dresses on the covers
of the tabloids beside her. "It's a girl. She's due February.
Valentine's."

"Oh, you know already, heh?" He tilted his head slightly

to the side and looked at her stomach. "So what name will you give to her?"

"Adale." Dominique felt the warm smile over her face again as she pulled her employee ID card from her wallet and handed it to him.

A smile lit his cheeks and he chuckled. "Oh, like in Africa, heh? What do you know about Adale? Have you ever been to Somalia?"

Dominique shook her head no with a spring and speed that surprised her, thrilled to talk to someone who knew about Adale, and who might know enough about the place to bring even more meaning to her daughter's name. "I seen it on T.V. though, and in the papers a long time ago. Is it pretty there? You been there? What's it like?"

He scanned her card and his smile faded. "You know, it's very bad over there right now. No water for so long, and then this."

It was not excitement, of course, Dominique would say she felt when she heard that Somalia had been affected by the tsunami . What welled in her stomach as the man told her about the devastation there was an ache, for sure. Yet whipped into the ache was a drizzle of reassurance, and something like pride that made Dominique want to smile and hide at once. She knew she should not be glad at all, yet the African man's terrible news affirmed her choice of her baby's name, and, therefore, the baby's destiny as she foresaw it. Listening to him, she grew surer and surer that Adale would not be forgotten; it would be part of the tickertape of numbers that had escalated all these days on the television screen. She imagined the piles of wrecked fishing boats he described laying along the beaches of Adale. She pictured the roads and wells he said had vanished into water after four years of sand-scratching draught. Dominique's stomach was stirred, moved in the direction of this man's story. She had felt close to that place for so long,

and now its name – her daughter's – would be for everyone
to know. It would appear, she was sure, on the screen beside
the pug-necked reporters, would be written in whatever
book as part of this, one of the most inconceivable and yet
undeniable times in history.

THE AIR ON the street had set into a deeper chill and a flatter
shade of gray. Dominique climbed the hill of 145th street as
steadily as she could, the pain still pinching her back and
now creeping outward and grabbing around her waist and
shoulders. The hedge of people in front of the Radio Shack
at the top of the hill had spread now into a larger mass of
coated forms, and two white men on ladders struggled to
attach a sign printed **RELIEF** over the building's skeletal
awning. Dominique approached, stepping away from the
front of this part of Harlem's best and most famous soul
food restaurant and into the street, the dull pain pulsing
over her hips as she stepped up onto the far curb.

Two brown-haired women stood in front of Dominique,
facing the folding table where three men sat behind bins of
white envelopes and two large water jugs, each filled a few
inches high with bills and change. Dominique had $6.51 in
her wallet, and not much more at home.

"And those children are so beautiful," a woman said as
she neared the table, pulling the cap from a shiny burgundy-
and-gold pen.

"Oh, I know. Absolutely gorgeous." The other dug into
a brown-roped purse Dominique recognized as a Louis
Vuitton.

When she got to the table, Dominique sat her oatmeal
upright beside the plastic jug. The man looked up at her
and smiled warmly, his pale white skin flushing red as a
breeze hit. "Would you like an envelope, or will you be
donating cash?"

"Cash." Dominique smiled back and opened her wallet. "To Adale."

"I'm sorry?"

"Somalia." She said. "I'm donating money for Somalia."

"I'm sorry, miss," he said, pressing his ungloved hands to his cheeks against the cold.

He told her that they would not be able to send donations to any specific country – that the money they raised would go to an organization whose name she recognized and who, he assured her with soft eyes, would provide aid for all the countries that needed it most. She thanked him, and asked for an envelope. After he told her that the envelopes were for check donations, and after she told him that she understood that and would like an envelope anyway, and a piece of paper as well, she slid a pen off of the table. The word spilled from her fingers to the paper as smoothly and beautifully as it had the first time she wrote it, and she hoped, she felt almost sure, in fact, that someone would read it, know what it was, what it meant. She slid the paper neatly into the envelope, the letters facing front, and stuffed her bills and change behind it.

As she turned away from the table, leaving the envelope in the hands of the man, whose face had tangled a little in mild confusion, Dominique heard the brunettes whispering.

"Somalia?" The woman's hands had disappeared into the pockets of her long gray coat, along with the pen, Dominique guessed.

"Yeah, I heard someone say there was some damage to the coast of Africa, too." The woman with the Vuitton huffed to her friend, looking flatly at Dominique flatly as she pushed by.

"Only 300 people died there, you know." The words

seemed to steam from the woman's mouth and hit the cement hard like a stream of hot piss on the corner.

Dominique parted her lips and began to think of something to say, but the women had rode the pavement away before she had a chance to respond, turning into the new Bank of America whose red, white and blue awning glowed into the street. Walking slowly after the women's clicking heels, Dominique considered this number, one she could more comfortably understand. She imagined the three hundred dollars she would find in her next and last pay check from her job in this place where she had lived her life and had her first child. She thought of the three hundred minutes she had spent in labor with Mandela, and the many cycles of three hundred sixty five days she had spent thinking of her children, planning for them and giving them what she could of what she thought they would need in the world. The plastic bag swung from her hands and knocked against her knees as she walked the long blocks back to the house, hoping that her mother and father would join them this morning for breakfast, and that Mandela had packed the last of his books.

X-24

MOHAMMED NASEEHU ALI

The Prophet of Zongo Street

I WAS NINE years old when I first met Kumi, who used to be one of our neighbors on Zongo Street, a densely populated section of Kumasi, Ghana's most prosperous city. Kumi was tall, lanky, handsome, and always well-dressed: clean white shirt, black tie, and neatly-pressed khaki trousers. He wore black shoes, and his strides were long and slow. His hair was nicely combed and he shaved every morning before he left home for the Central Post Office in the town proper, where he worked as a mail clerk.

Kumi lived by himself in an unadorned two-bedroom flat that was located at the dead end of Zongo Street. A low bamboo fence surrounded the flat, to keep pedestrians away. The fence was painted black, and so were the shutters of Kumi's flat; but for reasons known only to himself, Kumi

left the rest of the building unpainted. He was probably
the only person on our side of the street who liked flowers;
the hibiscus were his favorite, and planted them all over
his little compound.

Books were stacked everywhere inside Kumi's flat—
small books, large books, old books, and even antique
manuscripts that were entirely written by hand. The
windows of the flat were always shut, and the only source of
light in his living room was an old, rusty hurricane lantern
that sat on his study table. This always left the living room
in half-darkness, which he seemed to prefer. A large portrait
of his children—two boys of about the ages of seven and
nine—hung on the wall of Kumi's living room, though he
never talked about his children. There was speculation that
his wife had tried for months to seek a divorce from him
without any success and that he had come back home from
work one afternoon to an empty house. She had run away,
taking along their two sons. This had happened about two
years before Kumi moved to Zongo Street, when he used
to live in Ash Town, another suburb of the city. Mansa
BBC— the name we gave our street's biggest gossip, a large,
garrulous woman — claimed that Kumi's wife had run away
because she believed he was mad. Of course no sane person
on the street believed BBC's story, as every aspect of Kumi's
life seemed to reflect that of a full gentleman. And, besides
that, Kumi had never been seen talking aloud to himself or
running around naked in the market square, as some mad
people in town did.

Though Kumi's reticence and shyness made him quite
unapproachable, his generosity made him a favorite of
many people on Zongo Street. He seldom mixed with the
people, and yet he was respected by almost everyone: men
and women, adults and young children. His aloofness
was not because he was Western-educated and therefore
considered himself better than the streetfolks—a very

common trait among such types on Zongo Street and in the city. He was a person who humbly devoted himself to his books and his "thoughts" even though he did care for other people, especially the children in and around our neighborhood. On the few occasions Kumi mingled with people on the street—when he attended burial and funeral ceremonies—he sat far away from the crowd, in a corner, surrounded by little children, who were his best friends.

Unlike his fellow adults who gathered at Aliko's barber shop to engage in idle chatter, which usually ended in heated arguments, Kumi never argued or quarreled with anyone. He frequented the barber shop as often as twice each week, but he went only to get his hair trimmed; he never opened his mouth to join in the mindless arguments that went on. Kumi was always seen with his face buried in either a book or a newspaper, as if avoiding the stares of people on the street. He would lift up his head whenever someone greeted him and would say to the person: "How are you being treated by Fate?"

On Friday evenings he would invite me and my friends for a *biyan-tankwa* and biscuit party. And almost every day, on his way home from work, he bought for me, my brothers and sisters presents of meat-pies and Fanta drinks. My mother would thank Kumi when he brought the gifts to us, and at the same time she would ask him to stop buying such expensive food, insisting that it would spoil us.

At most of the weekly parties Kumi threw for me and my friends, he talked endlessly about the importance of education and the need to become good citizens of our community.

"You boys should take your studies seriously in order to become responsible adults in the future... you do not want to end up like Suraju," Kumi would say in his soft voice. Suraju was Zongo Street's most notorious swindler and petty thief; he was a drunkard as well. "All of you here know that Suraju would have led a decent life if he had had an education. It would have given him a decent job instead of the wretched life he is leading, sleeping all day long and getting up at night to steal and drink. Don't you agree with me?" Kumi would ask.

We would all reply "Yes," raising our fists in the air as if we really understood what he was talking about.

Kumi, at times, talked to us about Socrates, Nietzsche, Kant, and Spinoza. My friends and I had no idea who these people were—I didn't even know what the word philosophy meant at that time—but Kumi claimed that they were the greatest people who had ever lived and had tried, by means of their ideas, to recreate the world. He never explained to us why the ideas of these people failed. To be honest, Kumi's stories were quite boring at times, but we listened to them anyway—because of the food he gave us.

THE MORE I went to Kumi's flat, the more curious I became about his life; and it was partly because I never knew exactly what mood he was in at any given time. His face had an expression that showed neither sadness nor happiness; it did not resemble any form of sentiment I knew. I wondered what he thought about when he was alone in his flat and happened not to be reading.

Once when my friends and I were visiting Kumi, I asked him:

"Are you happy?"

Even before I finished the sentence, I realized how wrong it was of me, a mere child, to ask him such a question. At first I thought he would be upset and chide me, but in a friendly tone he asked: "Must one always be happy?"

I did not know what to say, and so I kept silent and looked away from him. For a while, Kumi did not say a word either, and I realized that he was waiting for me to speak. My friends sat uneasily, with a drawn and embarrased look on their faces.

After a brief silence, I stammered, "I.....I thought every person wants to be happy all the time. I want to.....I want to be happy all the time,"

Kumi smiled and began to speak.

"Listen carefully, Young Man, and all of you here as well." He moved his cane chair closer to where the four of us sat on the couch. "We human beings live every day of our lives in expectation of happiness." He paused, looked at me, and then continued. "But have you wondered why no son of Adam has ever attained complete happiness in his lifetime?" he asked, looking at us one by one.

We did not say a word. The truth was that we had nothing to say. We looked away from him and then at one another like a flock of sheep in a small, tight pen. I did not have any idea what my friends were thinking at that time, but, personally, I was already regretting that I had started the whole thing. Moments passed without any of us responding to Kumi's question, and so he continued.

"The reason we are never happy in life is that we are never content with what we have. The only means by which one could attain complete happiness is to avoid living in constant expectation of it. It's the expectation that causes our unhappiness and consequent bitterness about life." I did not know exactly what Kumi meant by that, but I went along with it all the same and nodded my head — as my friends did.

He then began a long discourse which Kumi concluded by saying, "Happiness is nothing but the comfort of illusion." *Happiness is nothing but the comfort of illusion?* I was hopelessly confused, and one of my friends was already dozing by the time Kumi got to this point in his lecture. As if trying to prevent us from leaving, Kumi quickly moved onto another topic—a topic on which he had often delivered long sermons to us.

"You must be able to restrict your utterances, Young Men, or else you and Trouble will forever dwell together. You should always remember that we human beings are what we say. Many times, greatly respected people have lost their dignity in the eyes of other people because they have allowed their mouths to precede their minds. Our egos may reside in our minds, but it is the mouth that makes it known to the rest of the world. So be mindful of what you say."

My friends and I were exhausted after Kumi's long sermon. Before we left his flat, he gave each one of us two toffees and encouraged us to visit again the next day.

During one of my numerous visits to Kumi, he told me that books are far better companions than human beings, because one learns from reading, and that unlike humans, books are reliable. Kumi spent his free time reading books that were as huge as the encyclopedias I saw in the Ashanti Library. He once told me that those books he read were books of theology. I didn't know what theology was, so I asked him what the books were really about. He told me that they were the lost books of Moses and all the Hebrew and Quraish apostles mentioned in the Bible and the Koran.

"Then how come you have them? Who gave these sacred books to you?"

"Don't worry, Young Man." he said, laughing. "This is beyond you now, but you'll understand later as you grow up."

As time went by, I gave up my attempts to understand Kumi, though I still visited his flat quite regularly. And then one evening he told me something that confused me more than ever. I didn't know whether to believe him or not. He told me that the history of the world was somehow fabricated by the white man.

"They changed everything in the original book of scriptures and filled it with false dogmas that suited their own greedy intentions," he said.

He also told me that the black race would have dominion over the rest of the world before it ends; he even claimed to know exactly when the world was going to come to an end. I asked him how he found that out.

"It was pre-determined," he replied. "The supreme ruler of the universe, in his revelation to Moses, predicted all of these and many other hidden truths, but they were altered."

"By whom?"

Kumi replied harshly: "Didn't you hear me? I said the white man!" Such harshness was quite unusual for him. He shoved a huge book in front of my face and asked me to read and find out for myself. Scared I quickly left, forgetting to take the book with me.

Later that day, after the evening meal, I told my mother about what Kumi had said to me, though I failed to mention his harsh attitude toward me. She said: "Do not go to his house so much. That man does not look healthy to me these days. He seems to be crazy in the head."

I silently disagreed with my mother, and I was, for a while, upset with her for speaking the way she did about my friend, though the dramatic change in him was evident. He stopped inviting us for drinks and biscuits on Friday nights, and also refrained from delivering presents to me and my sister. He no longer seemed to care so much about his neat appearance and demeanor in front of me and my friends, who rarely visited his flat by this time. The neatly stacked books in his living room were now scattered everywhere, making it difficult for one to even find space to put one's feet.

His hibiscus flowers began to wilt; the plants died in the end. Apparently he had not been watering them. But, despite all this, nothing Mother said about Kumi was enough to deter me from going to see him, who after nearly four years of friendship, had become one of the most important people in my life—moreso than even my *madrassa* and middle school teachers. I always came up with new excuses that would get me out of our house so that I could visit him. I would tell Mother that one of my friends had borrowed my textbook at school and that I was going to collect it. Before leaving our house, I would throw one of my books out through the window, so that I could carry it back with me, after I had visited Kumi.

On one of these visits, he looked me in the eye and said: "I am beginning a serious study of the history of mankind, and so I want you to stop coming here. I'll let you know when I am finished with my studies, so that you can start visiting again," he said, and rapped his fingers on my head. He gave me a little book that was entitled *Manifestations* and urged me to read it as soon as I could. I tried to read the book upon getting home that evening, putting aside my homework, but couldn't understand most of what I read. It was not until several weeks later—after reading and re-reading many sections of the book—that I finally began to get a grasp of its contents. It was written in 1932 by one Anthony Mtoli, a self-proclaimed "Africanist" and "Spiritualist" whom I had never heard of before. The book called for a universal black rebellion against "White dominance," and was full of curses and diatribes on Europeans, Arabs, and all white-skinned people. It was shocking and scary. I was brought up not only to revere Arabs and their culture, but to see each of them as a paragon of beauty, virtue, and spirituality. Islam was my religion, an Islam's prophet was himself Arab. At the *madrassa*, or Islamic school, I led to believe that all white people were geniuses and dare-devils, and that Arabs were divine among humans. And there I was, reading that some

"Arab Invaders" had once waged wars against black people in West Africa, and in the process of that war, had enslaved my ancestors and forced them to convert to Islam. For the first time I realized that there actually was a period in history when the people of my tribe, Hausa, weren't Moslems at all. Before I read *Manifestations*, I never doubted that humanity itself began with Islam, and that God had chosen a prophet among the Arabs because they were morally and spiritually superior to the rest of humankind.

Night after night before I went to sleep, I read and reread *Manifestations*. I was thirteen at the time, and the more I understood the book's contents, the more I thought about Kumi and wondered what he might be doing at that time. I was afraid to share my findings in the book with anyone, and eagerly awaited the day Kumi would come by and invite me to his flat again; I longed to impress him with my knowledge of the book he had given me. But my hope and excitement amounted to nothing. Fate had it that I was never to see the inside of Kumi's flat again.

DURING THE FIRST two months Kumi barred me from his flat, it was obvious that something was really bothering him, though no one could tell what it was. He walked hurriedly now, whispering to himself all the time, with no paper or book held to his face. He hardly responded to people's greetings anymore, including Mother's. As time went by, he was seldom seen on the street. I guessed he had stopped working at the Post Office as well, because one of his co-workers came to inquire about his continued absence.

One night, some six weeks after Kumi was last seen, we heard loud, piercing noises coming from his flat. And each night after that the noises grew louder and more intense. People began to gather in front of his flat at night to listen, although no one understood what the noises meant or what was actually going on inside. Rumor had it that the noises were made by the ghost of an old man, who, many years ago, was buried on the plot where Kumi's flat was erected. The noises sounded like the voices of a thousand people, all of them chanting, screaming, and shrieking. At one point, the street's imam gave an order that any person who valued his life should not go near the flat at night. As soon as it got dark, parents locked their children inside for fear of the bad spirits believed to be hidden in Kumi's flat. Even the adults, when they walked near the flat, did so in quick strides, as if they were being pursued.

The people on the street wished they could ignore the horrible noises, but it was impossible; they continued to get louder and more intense with the passing of each night. Meanwhile another rumor spread that Kumi had gone insane because he had read too many books. Yet another rumor suggested that he had died in his flat and that the noises were made by *his* ghost.

Then early one Friday morning—roughly three weeks after the noises had begun—we heard Kumi shouting. A handful of people came out to see what the matter was with him. They saw Kumi pacing up and down the street, holding a huge book, from which he recited. His normally clean-shaven face was now heavily bearded and his hair was curled into short, thick dreadlocks. Kumi had grown lean, almost skeletal. He was barefoot and was clad in a long white robe, with a red cotton belt tied around his thin waist.

Later that day, in the afternoon, people flocked into our neighborhood to listen to Kumi's sermons. For a while he was entertaining. He danced and chanted in praise of Ti-gari, whom Kumi claimed was the "supreme ruler of the universe." Kumi made gestures, shrieked, and stamped his feet on the ground in his spiritual delight.

"I am only a messenger," he cried. "For hundreds of

years you people have been led astray. You have been made to bow down to the images of false prophets and abstract gods, thinking that you are bowing down to the supreme ruler of the universe, Ti-gari himself. Look around you here. Look at the poverty in which you live; look at the misery, the ignorance, the disease. And yet you continue to worship their so-called omnipotent and beneficent Gods...The Christian slave traders told you that Jesus is the son of God, and this Jesus, according to them, is white. Meanwhile, the Islamic Invaders had already arrived and told our ancestors that it is because of the love of only one human being by the name of Muhammad that the world itself was created. You must remember that this Muhammad is supposedly white too, a white Arab."

Kumi claimed that everything he preached was revealed to him by the god of his new religion in nightly visions. It drove me close to tears when I stood among my junior secondary school mates and watched as he raved. I went up and tried to talk to him at the end of his first preaching session, but he acted as if I were a complete stranger to him. That night I cried silently before I went to sleep, careful not to let my mother hear.

"Long before these invaders came to our land, we had our own gods...gods of our ancestor's ancestors. We also had Ti-gari, who ruled over all the gods and men in this universe. Unlike the abstract and partial gods brought to us by these invaders, the gods of our ancestors and Ti-gari are merciful, generous, and impartial to the needs of people of all races—ours especially. Our ancestors used to live with these gods, and with Ti-gari himself. They talked face to face with the supreme ruler in their shrines, and all their needs were fulfilled. And then came the Moslems and Christians with their Gods! What did our ancestors do? They quickly abandoned their God, not knowing that these invaders had come to them with scriptures in one hand and a sword or chain hidden in the other, ready to capture and take them away. The Christian and Islamic intrusionists came and asked our ancestors to look up into the sky, to look up to heaven, while they filled their ships with our gold, young men and women, timber, diamond, cocoa—the list is endless. And even till this very day, we continue to allow them to strip us of our rightful and natural possessions that have been bequeathed to us by Ti-gari. Why can't we see the foolery? Why can't we see the falsity? Why do we continue to take this insult? Why?" Kumi at times seemed to lack answers for some of his own profound questions.

People turned out in great numbers during the early days of his preaching. And while some of them were inclined to believe in Kumi's new religion, others thought he had gone mad or that his behavior was the result of heavy drinking.

"According to the scriptures they brought to you, Jesus is said to have hair like lamb's wool," Kumi shouted during an afternoon of preaching. "Now, you all know what a lamb's wool looks like. Just like your hair and my hair, right? Why then? Why didn't we question the Europeans when they brought us the blonde-haired and blue-eyed pictures of Jesus, telling us that he is the son of their God? And why didn't we question the Arabs, who bought and sold our ancestors into slavery, while preaching to us that their religion is one of peace and equality? Because you know what, Brothers and Sisters? It was because we allowed our minds to be carried away by false promises of gold, wicked glory, and an eternal redemption that is nothing but a hoax!"

Kumi knelt down at this point, and from his bag he pulled out a portrait of a man he claimed to be the real Jesus, and whose true name according to him was I'sama. He raised up the portrait—which was drawn on a piece of cardboard paper—so that everyone present could see. The figure in the portrait had overgrown bushy hair, a flat nose, prominent lips, and was dark-skinned. He returned the portrait to his bag after a short while, and then continued with his preaching. "And so, Brothers and Sisters, do not bow down to any false images of I'sama. He is a servant of Ti-gari and not a son of any of their Gods as they made you to believe. And remember always that he is as black as anyone among you here."

I did not know what to think of Kumi's new religion, which he called Afromadiya. I asked my mother's opinion about it, and all she said to me was, "Too much knowledge at times leads people to the ways of the devil." She then warned me to stay completely away from Kumi. I began to think that he might actually be evil. And yet I refused to believe all the speculation that went on about him, and argued with school mates of mine who believed him mad.

In her bid to console me about Kumi's plight, Mother told me that people who were crazy had the same capacity to create justifications for their behavior that normal people did. I realized that her explanation—as rational as it seemed—was probably intended to make me understand how hopeless Kumi's situation was, and thereby help me to come to terms with it. Her attempt, however, had the opposite effect on me: I developed an even greater feeling of pity for Kumi, saying to myself that he was a victim of a power or force I did not know.

Then things began to get worse for poor Kumi. His body began to smell, apparently because he had stopped taking his bath. He was obviously not eating, as he grew thinner and thinner. Some of the kinder people on the street, including a few of his relatives who lived on Zerikyi Road, tried to talk Kumi out of his new occupation, but he refused to listen to anyone. Some even attempted to send him to the mental asylum in the town proper, but he cursed and threatened them, saying that whoever touched him would be afflicted with an incurable disease. In the end, he was left alone.

Despite Kumi's deteriorating health, he still remained unrelenting in his attempt to spread the new religion. And by this time, seven months into his vocation as a preacher, everyone on the street had lost interest in listening to what Kumi had to say, with the exception of the children who took him as a mere entertainer. After a while, however, even the children got tired of listening to Kumi's exhortations. But that did not discourage him from preaching, which he did day and night, rain or shine. Gradually, his voice grew thin, almost inaudible. People began to walk past him without even looking at him. He, meanwhile, remained the only known convert to this new religion.

Then one day during the rainy season, there came a terrible storm. The wind that followed the rain ripped off the roofs of many buildings on Zongo Street. It rained continuously for three days and nights, with thunder and lightning, as if the whole world was coming to an end. While people were in their houses during this storm—praying for the protection of their lives and property—Kumi was outside preaching to no one but himself. We would peep through our windows and would see him pacing up and down the muddied street, still preaching, his voice drowned out by the pounding rain.

After this fateful storm Kumi was not seen on the street for a couple of days. I had a feeling that some terrible thing had happened to him, but I had no idea what it might be. Two nights after the storm, I had a dream, and in that dream I saw Kumi being lifted up into the sky by black angels. I told my mother about this dream the following morning, but she hushed me up and warned me not to disclose "this ominous dream" to anyone, not even my father.

On the third day after the storm, while people were

still trying to repair their damaged roofs and fences, some concerned neighbors decided to find out what had happened to Kumi. These neighbors, including my father, knocked several times on Kumi's door, but heard no response. A day was allowed to pass, in the hope that he would come out if he were in his flat, but this hope ended in vain.

Five days passed, and Kumi was still not seen. The street's elders then decided that his flat must be broken into. It did not take my father and the others much effort to break into the flat, because they found the main door unlocked. They pushed it open and walked inside. Kumi was found lying on his bed, pale and quite dead. He was still clad in his white robe, and the red cotton belt was tied tightly around his thin waist. And out on the street people whispered darkly that a book, a very large one, lay open on his chest.

Everything about Kumi's funeral was carried out hastily. Instead of the three to seven days that were usually spent to mourn and pray for the dead, not even a full day was spent for him. And not many people showed up at the funeral either, not even his run-away wife and two children. A handful of his relatives from Zerikyi Road and about a dozen people from the street made up the entire gathering at the prayer ceremony; and they could barely wait for the imam's closing prayers, so that they could leave and attend to their personal affairs.

Parents on the street forbade their children to go near the place where Kumi's funeral was being held, claiming that his ominous death might bring ill-luck to their families. But despite this fear, my father took me along with him. I sat on a short stool the whole time the prayers were being recited, with my mind not on the imam's words but on the book that Kumi had given to me, the little book that had not only revealed to me the highest truth about humanity but had also taught me things I never before knew about myself,

my family, clan, tribe, and race. I wondered if my father
had ever read such a book, and what his thoughts might
have been about it. But I dared not ask Father questions like
that—even a fourteen year old like me wasn't supposed to
ask questions anyway, especially if those questions raised
doubts about Islam and any of our traditions. So I walked
silently behind my father after the prayers, anxious to
reach home so that I could read aloud, as a memoriam,
passages from *Manifestations*, which was at that time tucked
in between the skin of my belly and the waist band of my
khaki shorts.

X-24

unclassified

GAYLENE GOULD

The Sacrifice

JESSE WAS MID-CYCLE the day the plan was executed. Ritualistically, she noted it in her diary – the number 14 penned in a perfect pink circle. Exactly fourteen days since the beginning of her last period, exactly fourteen days till the next. Page ninety-four of *GCSE Double Science* warned her to expect feelings of excess energy. She'd be needing it today, she fancied.

Because Frankie said they had to do everything as normal that day, she spent the afternoon with the girls swapping sentimental stories about their first encounters with a penis. Catching your first peek at seven meant you were pretty late to the game, Jesse discovered, which didn't surprise her as she was late to the game most of the time. Five of them, sprawled out in Saturday afternoon ease, bounced Jack, Melanie Jones's four-month old baby, on their laps.

Jesse, fuelled by excess energy and adrenaline, surprised everyone by acting out her episode. She improvised the time she'd been playing down by the dumps with her best friend Kalavati when the old man who walked his Alsatian dog sauntered by. He had nonchalantly waved his usual hello before flipping it out like a party trick. It was shock that had caused her breath to catch on a giggle - that and the sight of Kalavati's plaits swinging like two jump ropes as her friend took off with high speed up the lane. Jess had glanced back to catch the old man's upright member and his ridiculous how-about-that-then grin and found her knees buckling with the hilarious, outrageous banality of it all.

The girls guffawed on cue and she felt her chest swell. She had been testing her toes in the tepid pool of their caustic reaction for a while now so this result pleased her. She'd served her story the way they liked them served, feisty and fearless. Sticking two fingers up to your rotten past was how most at Ryders Children's Home survived it. Weeping over bruises like a baby girl was not acceptable. Jesse's recovery from the shock of her grandmother's vanishing grip had been slow and only recently had she caught herself relaxing into the disorientating, limitless freefall that was Ryders.

Melanie rolled her eyes and lengthened her long body out along the floor tucking her arm under her head. As she mono-toned in her practised drawl, something about her dad shaving naked in the bathroom while her little heels kicked against the cold toilet bowl, Jesse mentally noted that men's private parts weren't that private at all.

YOU COULDN'T TELL that Melanie had had a baby - everybody said so. Jesse found it hard to pull her eyes away from Melanie's tummy with the little glittering belly stud. It was tight as ever. That's breastfeeding for you Melanie had said and Jesse found her eyes travelling up to where used to hang two huge watermelon breasts but now slouched two melon-sized mammaries. While Jesse was discovering her first pubic hair, Melanie's body had shape-shifted into a full grown woman's. At 16 she was only three years older than Jesse but an entire ocean of experience separated them. Melanie had carried a nine-pound weight in the front of her belly skin and had pushed it out through the tiny hole that Jesse daren't yet broach with a tampon applicator but more amazing than all that, Melanie had had sex , with a man, and probably more than once.

She had learned on page one-three-six of *GCSE Double Science* that it was overheated blood forcing its' way through straining capillaries that stimulated an erection and that some strange force called libido caused the blood to rush faster. But because there were no diagrams of it, Jesse had no idea what a libido looked like. Melanie, however, seemed to have attuned her body to this elusive knowledge. Even before she left Ryders, Melanie had walked and talked like she had existed on the planet for thousands of years. She swished dark mascara on her eyelashes while her bottom lip hung loose, absently reeling off the names of men that she was in the process of avoiding. She hung out with the older girls and during the darkening winter afternoons, they would arrange themselves along the outside wall, not speaking, looking out, as the lights from car headlamps made movie premiere arcs across them. Soft shoulders leaning back, rounding hips thrust outward, it was as if their taut bodies and blank faces were psychically separated. Jesse would watch from the window growing frustrated as cars would crawl up and the girls would pretend not to notice. To Jess, they seemed to possess an inexplicably alluring, scientifically incalculable Amazonian mystery.

THERE WAS ONLY one time that Jess felt a deep twinge of recognition with the alien that was Melanie. It was the time

Melanie was forced to leave, because of Jack, and her dad came to pick her up in his car. He was silently standing gripping the open passenger door staring straight above his approaching daughter's head. Melanie, with her big belly, waddled towards him studying her feet. It was like watching her final steps to the gallows. After they drove away, Jesse realised that Melanie and her dad hadn't said two words to each other and it was the only time that Melanie had appeared like Jess always felt, an awkward child.

AFTER THE MY First Penis confessions, came the definitive topic of pervy conversation, Mad Max. Jesse's tummy somersaulted in nervous anticipation. It was inevitable the conversation would take this turn. It always did when the girls were alone. Mad Max kept the newsagents on the corner and spent most of his working life hoarding his takings in the back room and pretending to stock shelves while following school girls with hungry eyes. Most Ryders' girls, like Rebecca Longbottom, harboured many a sordid Mad Max tale.

Rebecca was telling of the time that she and Jesse had passed by the shop after school.

"Remember Jess? Remember?"

Jess could never, probably ever, forget.

"Right. Me and Jess were coming from school, right, and Jess was gabbling on as usual something about her and Frankie and TT. Anyways I wanted to go and get some sweets right so I left Jess outside and went in on my own. Well, and you know what he's like. Na-aa-sty, so anyways I go to pick up some sweets and he's like "Can I help you?" and I'm thinking "Yeah I bet you wanna help" so he comes over, right Jess? He comes right over and he pushed his hard bony thing right up against my back!"

On cue the girls yucked and fell on their faces, their

cheeks burning, passing each other sidelong glances. Rebecca had risen and was acting out the action with over-exaggerated hip thrusts.

"And the thing is, the thing is right all I can see is Jess standing outside looking through the window with her mouth dropped so wide you could've driven the Number 22 through it!"

The shrieks reached to number five on the Richter scale but Jess didn't hear. She didn't count on Rebecca telling this private moment, this secret that should only be re-run in slow motion in the quiet dark. Jess couldn't stop the well worn spool unravelling in her head. Rebecca sashaying slowly past Max, the angle of her head and chest high, the long red hair trailing her waist, Max's mouth open, Jesse's breath frozen on the glass, Rebecca gliding between rows of mushy peas and aging sherbet dip packets, Max spell bound, as if one more switch of Rebecca's red hair would cause him to explode leaving nothing but a pair of steaming shoes. It was a grotesque, titillating scene, Jesse outside, impatient, a feeling of delicious dread hanging in the pit of her stomach. At that precise moment Jesse had learnt the secret behind that Amazonian prowess that had so eluded her, the formula missing from the Biology text book that changed girls to women. And it lay in the place that Jess would never have thought to look. It lay in a gaze, a man's gaze and even if you couldn't reach inside his head, just watching him watching you could alter you. At thirteen she was ready for that transformation, for Frankie to witness it, to watch him watching her with that funny feeling of delicious dread churning up his stomach.

**

MELANIE WAS LOOKING through the window and pulling a face.

"Jess, it's your boyfriend."

Jesse jumped up and peered through a crack in the musty smelling curtain. Franklyn, TT and Orphan were traipsing up the path, the knuckles of their football boots crunching on the gravel. Other boys were ambling past the wall, shouting the end to trailing conversations. As Franklyn reached the step, he peeled off his sweaty shirt and Jesse caught sight of his lean glistening back and the dip that disappeared into the top of his tracksuit bottoms.

The dreams of touching Frankie's body had begun to invade her waking hours so she hardly caught Melanie's loose comment.

"He's fit, but stuck up" she pronounced just as Frankie looked up toward them. Jesse quickly stepped back. "He's turning sixteen soon ain't he? You two done it yet?"

Jesse, again, thanked her dark skin for cloaking the deep blush that surged through her body. Not from want of trying, she commented soundlessly, before Melanie, in an uncharacteristic bout of sensitivity, moved the conversation along to an equally inflammable topic.

"Sixteen eh? They'll be kicking him out soon? What's he gonna do then?"

The hot blush turned to a cold flash and before she could check it, Jess shot out.

"Don't you worry about me and Frankie. We got plans."

Maybe it was how she said it but the girls looked up at her with raised eyebrows. Frankie was urgently beckoning her from outside, his face dark and brooding.

"I've got to go."

"Ooh when Frankie calls Jess drops everything".

That was the last thing Jesse heard as she bounced out the room.

***

"WE ONLY HAVE ourselves in the world."

Frankie was fingering the postcard again. The sellotape that sealed in the colourful magazine collage was wearing on the edges.

Orphan was gently driving through the high street, his hands at a sedate ten to two, trying to look all of eighteen and responsible. This was not the day to draw attention to themselves.

She didn't want them to feel this tension. She didn't want them to worry. They were all she had in the world. She could tell TT was staring at her even though she was concentrating on the grey passing street life. He often looked at her in secret like this. Without turning, she slyly pinched the back of his hand and he responded by tickling her palm. She turned to look at Frankie in the front seat, the only one who mattered. Soon he would be sixteen and forced to leave Ryders and even though the children's home was not ideal, it was the extent of their known universe. Without it, a chasm opened up in front of them. So Frankie's vision of the future became their own and his plan was the lifeline that would take them there. Frankie was staring hard at the postcard.

"Tell us about it again Frankie."

It was the only way to calm him. He leaned back and stretched as if he had already reached.

"See it deh? Here's you and me Jess walking on the beach."

He pointed to two slender white bodies caught in mid-motion stepping on brilliant white sands. Stuck on top of their bodies were blurred oversized photographs of Frankie and Jesse's heads. The sea lapping by their feet was a suspicious turquoise blue.

"That there says Antigua and that cross on the top of that hill is your granny's grave and here's TT and Orphan's big heads standing by their 4x4. See how white the sand is and how green the trees are? Bwoy."

The postcard had once innocently depicted a tranquil Caribbean beach scene but was now busied up with mis-matched photos and magazine cut-outs, defaced by crude biro markings. Jesse had never seen a work of art so beautiful.

"Hey Frank," Orphan smiled, rolling down the window to throw his cigarette butt out. "Why'd you have to stick our heads onto white people's bodies?"

"Listen blood YOU try and find a Caribbean postcard with black people on the beach, you get me?"

They laughed. They laughed until the sound drained out and only tears were left and Jess felt it again, the unrestrained purity of what existed between them. They were all she wanted in life – TT, Orphan and most of all Frankie. He turned to look at her and not for the first time, she felt her heart stop for a moment. Even *GCSE Double Science* couldn't explain such a tender heart attack.

By the time the last long sigh had been breathed, they had pulled to a gentle stop opposite Mad Max's shop. Then they were still, examining the flat nondescript window as if it was the ceiling of the Sistine Chapel.

"So WE ALL got it right?"

Frankie lit a cigarette and began to outline the plan for the last time, his eyes fixed on the window.

"Just remember this is our ticket outta here. We can be gone by the end of the week. Missing. Laters. This is just a natural bizness. TT you been cracking safes since the year dot. And, Orphan, God blessed you with the gift to drive cars fast. How's he gonna not expect you to pull this kinda shit?"

Orphan tried a laugh.

"And me with my mad lock picking skills ….." He kept his eyes trained, trained away. "And Jess….."

He took a long, slow drag on the cigarette. His fingers were genteel and tapered like a lady's and even from the back seat she could see the curve of his lashes.

"Dirty pervert, how's he gonna call the Boys if he's got an underage in the shop. That's what you said init Jess? Jess, you our living protection. All we need is ten minutes girl. You just gotta keep him busy for ten minutes. That's all. Did you wear it?"

Jesse slowly peeled back her grey school cardigan. Underneath was the tight see-through shirt that Frankie had picked and bought especially for her. Orphan gagged on an 'oh shit' and TT looked away.

Frankie turned to face her. His eyes were soft and doe-like.

"This is a just natural bizness," he said looking right at her.

He turned away to face the window again and drew deeply on his cigarette.

"We ready?"

***

THE WALK FROM the car to the shop doorway was interminably long, but Jess didn't mind. She switched her hips this way and that like she was on a catwalk. TT said he would leave the door to the storeroom open so they could watch. And she knew what to do, how to sashay, how to thrust her hips out, how to raise her chest and stick her bottom out so it was high and round. And she *would* perform it, perform it with all her heart.

X-24

Daniel Alarcón

Republica and Grau

THE BLIND MAN lived in a single room above a bodega on a
street not so far away. It was up a slight hill, but then so was
everything in the neighborhood. Maico was ten years old
when they met. There was nothing on the walls of the blind
man's room, nor was there anywhere to sit, and so Maico
stood. A single bed, a night stand with a radio wrapped in
duct tape, a washbasin. The blind man had graying hair
and was much older than Maico's father. The boy looked
at his feet, and swept together a small mound of dust from
the cement floor while his father and the blind man spoke.
The boy didn't listen, but then no one expected him to. He
was not surprised when a tiny black spider emerged from
within the insignificant pile he had made. It skittered across
the floor and disappeared beneath the bed. Maico raised

his eyes. A cobweb glittered in an upper corner. It was the room's only decoration.

His father reached out and shook the blind man's hand. "So it's agreed," Maico's father said, and the blind man nodded, and this was all.

A WEEK LATER, they were in the city, at the noisy intersection of Republica and Grau. They had risen early on a winter morning of low, leaden clouds, and made their way to the center, to this place beneath the shadow of a great hotel, amid the snarling, bleating traffic. The blind man carried a red-tipped cane with him, and he knew the route well, but once they had arrived, he folded his cane and left it in the grassy median. His steps became tentative and Maico understood that the pretending had begun. The blind man's smile disappeared and his jaw went slack.

Everything there was to know Maico learned in that first hour. The timed lights, the three minutes of working followed by three of waiting. Maico's mother hadn't wanted him to work in the city, had said so the previous night, but his father bellowed and slammed a fist on the table. Of course, these gestures were hardly necessary, and in truth, Maico didn't mind the work. He even liked the pace, especially those moments when there was nothing to do but watch the endless traffic, soak in the dull roar of it, the sound of a horn, or twenty horns, and the looks of all those people with places to go in the urgent city. "Grau connects the center to the northern districts," the blind man explained. He had the city mapped clearly in his mind. There was money to be made in the north: it was a land of people trying to better themselves. Not like the southern rich who had forgotten where they'd come from. "The north is different," the blind man said. "It's a generous intersection, this one. These people look at me and they remember me and love me because they have known me their entire lives.

They *give*."

Maico listened as well as he could amid the din. Me me me – that was what he heard. The cars and the engines and the blind man; it was all one sound. Acrid fumes hung over the intersection, so toxic that after only an hour Maico could feel a bubble in his chest, and then, in his throat, something tickling.

He coughed and spat. He apologized, as his mother had taught him.

The blind man laughed. "You'll do much worse here, boy. You'll cough and piss and shit and it will all be the same."

And this was the work: when the traffic stopped, the blind man kept one hand on the boy's shoulder, with the other stretched out his tin, and together they walked up the row of idling cars. Maico led him toward the cars with rolled down windows, and the blind man muttered helplessly as he approached each one. Maico's only job was to steer him toward those who were likely to give, and make sure he did not waste time on those who would not. Women driving alone were, according to the blind man, preemptively generous, hoping, in this way, to avoid being robbed. They kept small coins in their ashtrays for just such transactions. This was city life, after all. Taxi drivers could be counted on as well, because they were working people, and men with women always wanted to impress and so might let slip a few coins to show their sensitive side. Men driving alone rarely gave, and not a moment should be squandered before a car with tinted windows. "If they know you can't see them," the blind man said, "they don't feel shame."

"But they know *you* can't see them," Maico said.

"And that's why you're here."

The clouds would thin by noon, but that morning was cool and damp. The blind man kept all the money, periodically announcing how much they had collected. It wasn't much. Each time a coin was dropped in, the blind man bowed humbly, and though he had not been not asked to, Maico did the same. The blind man emptied the tin into his pocket when the light changed, and told Maico to look out for thieves, but the boy saw only men hawking newspapers and chalkboards, women who carried baskets of bread or flowers or fruit, and the very fullness of the area made it seem safe. Everyone had been kind to him so far. A woman his mother's age gave him a piece of bread with sweet potato because it was his first day. She tended to a few toddlers in the median, and they played with a stuffed animal, taking turns tearing it to pieces. The woman seemed to encourage them. The stuffing spread over the grass in white clumps, and when a truck rolled by, these were blown into the street.

Maico could not tell what kind of animal it had been.

When the blind man found out Maico had been to school, he bought a newspaper, and had the boy read it to him. He nodded or clucked his teeth while Maico read, and the stories were so absorbing that they even missed a few lights to finish hearing them. A judge had been murdered the previous day, in broad daylight, at a restaurant not far from where they sat. An editorial defended the life of a guard dog the authorities wanted put down for having killed a thief. There would be a new president soon, and protests were planned to welcome her. Music leaked from the windows of passing cars, now from buses, and Maico could hear voices at each stop light singing along to a dozen different melodies. When he could, he studied the blind man's face. Unshaven and olive-skinned, with puffy cheeks; his nose was crooked and squat. He didn't wear dark glasses as some blind do, and Maico could guess that the sullen sheen of his useless gray eyes was part of his worth as a beggar. It was a competitive area after all, and there were others working that morning whose qualifications for the position were clearly beyond question.

His father was waiting at the door of the blind man's room when they came home that afternoon. He winked at Maico, and then greeted the blind man gruffly, surprising him. "The money," he said, with no warmth in his voice. "Let's see it."

The blind man pulled out his key and patted the door for the lock. "Not here. Inside is better. You people with eyes are always so impatient."

And Maico stood by while they divided the take. He noticed the spider had added to his lonely creation. The counting went slowly. The blind man felt each coin carefully, then announced its worth out loud. When no one contradicted him, he continued, his hands moving with elegant assurance, organizing the money into piles on his bed. A few times he misidentified a coin, but Maico felt certain this was by design. The third time it happened, Maico's father sighed impatiently. "I'll count," he said, but the blind man would have none of it.

"That wouldn't be fair, now would it?"

When it was finished, Maico and his father walked home in silence. It had taken longer than they had expected, and Maico's father was in a hurry. His mother asked how it had gone, and his father sneered and said there was no money. Or none worth mentioning, and don't bother me, woman.

He prepared for his night shift while the boy and his mother ate dinner without him.

The second day it was the same, and on the third, when they were walking down the hill, Maico's father took the boy to the market and bought him a soda. An old gentlemen with thick, calloused hands served them. Maico drank his soda through a straw; his father poured his into a glass. He asked his son how the work was, whether he liked it, and by now Maico was old enough to know he should not say too much. He'd learned from his mother.

Did he like downtown?

He did.

And was he enjoying the work?

He was.

What was it like, and here, Maico chose his words carefully, explaining what he absorbed in these few days. About charity, about traffic, about the relative generosity of cards headed north versus those headed south.

Maico's father listened calmly. He finished his soda, ordered a beer, then thought better of it. He looked at his watch, then scattered a few coins on the counter, and the old man swept them into his palm with a frown. "We're being robbed," Maico's father said. "Do you hear me, boy? You've go to keep track of the money, you've got to add it up in your head."

Maico was quiet.

"Are you listening to me? The blind man gets half. We get half."

The blind man had bought Maico a bag of popcorn that morning. Maico read him the paper, and the blind man told him stories about the city when the air was sweet, when it had not been so noisy. The place he'd described seemed fantastical. "Even the intersection where we work was quiet once," the blind man had said, and he'd smiled because he knew this was unbelievable.

Now the boy looked up at his father.

"You can't let a blind man hustle you, son," his father said. "It's an embarrassment."

Maico did his best to keep an accurate count the next day, but by lunchtime the exhaust made him swoon. When Maico asked, the blind man said he couldn't know for sure.

"I'll count it later," he said.

"Count it now," Maico said. The words came out with a certain snap that the boy liked.

But the blind man just smiled. "Cute," he said. "Now read the next story."

A horn blew and then another, and soon it was a chorus. When the street was quiet enough, Maico opened the paper again. An entire village in the mountains had been poisoned during a festival. Bad meat. The Minister of Health was airlifting in medicine and doctors. He meant to read further, but the light changed, and it was time to work.

Every afternoon Maico's father was there to meet them at the door of the blind man's room. The money was never enough, and his father could not or would not hide his displeasure. Maico could sense it, knew with such certainty it was coming, that when on the eighth day his father knocked the radio off the nightstand and said, "you stealing blind fuck," he felt he had willed it to happen. His father, angry, was a sight to behold: the great red face of him, eyes open to the whites, fists like steel mallets. Maico wondered if the blind man could truly appreciate the spectacle. Was his father's voice, the sharp edge of it, enough?

If nothing else, the blind man understood the seriousness of the moment. He seemed neither surprised nor afraid when his pockets were emptied.

The radio sputtered and died.

Until it stopped, Maico hadn't even noticed it was on.

THEY WERE BACK at work a few days later, with a new agreement. The boy would keep the money now. "I'm going to let you hold it," the blind man said, but Maico knew it was his father who decided how things would be. The money weighed heavy in his pocket, so that it felt like a lot more than it was. Just coins. Small, old, thin coins, worthless, worn-down coins, and when the work was done that day, the blind man asked the boy to point him toward the hotel. It was sunny, and in the slanting afternoon light the hotel's glowing glass exterior seemed to be made of gold. "Now let's walk to it," the blind man said. He knew the way, but here, in front of their regular clientele, it was understood that the boy should continue to lead him. They crossed Grau together, the blind man's hand on Maico's shoulder.

"On the far side of the hotel is a street. Read me the sign," the blind man said.

It was a narrow street. "Palomares," Maico said.

"Let's walk down this one, boy. Away from Grau."

When they had crossed the second intersection, the blind man asked what was on each corner. Maico went clockwise: a bakery, a man selling roasted corn from a cart, an internet café, a butcher shop.

The blind man smiled. "Behind the cart, what is there?"

"A bar."

"This bar – what's it called?"

"El Moíses."

"Let's go in."

Afternoon, quiet in the bar, and the blind man asked Maico to choose the very best table. The boy picked one by a window. El Moíses was just below street level, and so the windows allowed a view of people's legs as they passed by. The smell of roasted corn on the cob filled the bar, and they hadn't been there long before the blind man gave in and asked for two. He'd already finished his first beer by then. He gave one ear of corn to Maico, and washed his down with a second cold glass of beer. He spoke wistfully of the fights he had come across in this very same space: of chairs thrown, of bottles broken and brandished as weapons, of the beautiful noise of conflict. You could hear it in the breathing of those around you – panic, fear, adrenaline. There were a dozen names for that extraordinary sensation.

"What do you do when it happens?" Maico asked.

"Well, you fight, of course."

"But what do *you* do?"

"Ah, that's what you mean. How does a blind man fight? I'll tell you." He smiled and spoke nearly in a whisper. "Recklessly. With whatever implement is at hand. Swinging wildly and searching desperately for an exit." The blind man sighed. "I suppose it's not so different for those who can see. More desperate perhaps, or more reckless."

The waiter had turned on a radio, a low humming melody that Maico could not make out. They were the only people in the bar.

"Tell me," the blind said after awhile, "what do you look like? I should have asked sooner. Describe yourself."

No one had ever asked Maico such a thing. In fact, it wouldn't have occurred to him that a question like that could even be asked. Describe himself. He thought for a moment, but nothing came to mind. "I'm a boy," he managed. "I'm ten years old."

"More than that," the blind man said. He took a swig from his beer. "I need more than that."

Maico squirmed in his chair.

"What does your face look like? I know you're small for your age. How are you dressed?"

"Normal," is all the boy could say. "I'm dressed normal. I look normal."

"Your pants, for example, or your shirt – what material are they?"

"I don't know."

"Can I touch it?" the blind man said, but without waiting for an answer he had already reached out and was testing the fabric of Maico's shirt between his thumb and forefinger. "Is the color very faded?"

"No," Maico said.

"Does your shirt have a collar?"

"Yes."

"Are there holes in the knees of your pants?"

"They're patched."

"And are they hemmed?"

"Yes."

The blind man grunted. "Your shirt is tucked in?"

Maico looked down. It was.

"And you're wearing a belt, I assume. It's leather?"

"Yes."

The blind man sighed. He called for another beer, and when the glass was placed on the table, the blind man asked the waiter to stay for a moment. "Sir, excuse me," he said, raising his right hand. He told Maico to stand and then addressed the waiter again. "How would you describe the general appearance of this child?"

The waiter was a serious, unsmiling man. He looked Maico over, from head to toe. "He's dressed neatly. He looks clean."

"His hair. Is it combed?"

"Quite."

The blind man thanked him, and invited Maico to sit once again. He drank his beer, and for a moment Maico thought the blind man wouldn't speak again. A new song started up, a voice accompanied by a bright, ringing guitar, and the blind man smiled and tapped his fingers against the table. He sang along, tra-la-laed for a moment when he didn't know the words, and then fell silent altogether.

"Your old man thinks he's a tough guy," he said finally, after the song had finished and the waiter had brought him another beer. "Here's the problem. He goes off to work every night, and doesn't see you in the morning, and meanwhile, your mother dresses you. She must be a nice woman. Very correct. But you're a momma's boy. Pardon me, son, but I must speak plainly. That's why we don't make money. You can't beg looking like this."

Maico was silent.

The blind man laughed. "Are you taking this hard?"

"No," said Maico.

"Good. Very well." The blind man nodded and whistled for the waiter, who appeared at the table and announced what was owed.

"Thank you, sir," the blind man said, smiling in every direction. "A receipt, please. The boy will be paying."

THAT NIGHT HIS father went into a rage. Where's the money, where's the money, you lazy little shit, and what could he say except this: I spent it, the sentence escaping on its own, and his fear arrived as soon as these three words and the half-truth they expressed were audible. Fear spread outward from his chest so that his arms felt light and useless, his stomach watery, and then his legs would not hold him up any longer. His mother, when she tried to intervene, was beaten as well, and there was a moment in that short, furious episode – an instant – when Maico felt certain he would not survive. His mother's screams let him know that this was worse than before, not like the other times, although if he had dared open his eyes, he might have guessed the same from the savage look on his father's face. You what? Then there was noise and there was light and Maico peeked and the room itself seemed to move. He was pushed and he stood and he was shoved and he surprised himself by standing again and this continued until he could no longer could. His mother wailed, begging, praying aloud to the saints while Maico felt the walls about to collapse, and heat as if from a great, exhaling fire.

All was quiet. He didn't know how much time had passed, only that his father had gone. Maico opened his eyes. The glass door of the cabinet had been shattered, a chair leg snapped. It was a storm, and now it had passed; inexplicably, there was no blood. His mother leaned against the far wall, not sobbing, just breathing, and Maico crawled toward her, and then he slept.

Maico didn't dream that night. The few hours of sleep he managed were blank, dark, and without stories. He woke at dawn in his bed. His mother must have moved him.

The blind man arrived the next morning, as if nothing had happened. Maico saw him and realized he'd expected the man had been killed, that the fury his father had unleashed on him and on his mother would have been doubled or tripled for the blind man. Instead the blind man wore the same contented look he'd had the previous afternoon when he left the boy at the bus stop downtown, saying he would make his own way home. There had been a softness to his words, not drunk, Maico knew, but happy, as happy as Maico was humiliated, as happy as Maico was angry.

"Go," his mother said. "Go, we need the money," and so Maico swallowed, and stretched his sore, wounded body. He stared angrily at the blind man, thinking to himself that such a useless act had never felt so necessary, and then, with his mother sighing softly, he went.

Maico knew the way by then. Knew it well. Knew the names of the streets they passed on their descent to the center, the turns they took, the intersections where the road rutted and the bus shook. All the sights along the way, the determined faces of the men and women who got off and on, and the collective breath the bus took as they crossed the bridge just before the old center. In the rainy season, the thin, dirty stream beneath them would come to life – or a kind of life – but for now it was an anemic trickle that would not make it to the sea. Boys his age ran along the riverbed; Maico could see them from the bus, tending to their oily fires. If he'd been asked, he could have described it all for the blind man, this city of dirt and smoke, but Maico supposed the blind man knew this place better than he ever would. He didn't read the paper that day, did not listen to the blind man's stories as the avenue filled and emptied according to its own somber rhythms. He waited for the blind man to apologize, though he knew it wouldn't happen. He didn't bother to count the money before it disappeared into his pocket, and it was only when the skies had cleared, with the sun pouring through a gaping hole in the clouds, that he realized there had never been so much. Maico touched his face. His sore jaw, his bruised cheek, his right eye, not swollen shut, but pinched so that he had to strain to keep it open. The blind man couldn't know. Describe yourself. Whatdoyoulooklike.

Beggar.

He was surrounded by them, could see them now: this itinerant army of supplicants, these salesman who were really the same thing, these many waiting for a stroke of good luck, for some generous act to redeem the day or the week or the month. Counting, hour after hour, the careful arithmetic of survival, this much for food, this much if I walk home, this much for the children, for the house, for the soup, for the drink, for the roof over my head. This much to keep the cold at bay. Maico's father spent his waking hours in another part of the city, engaged in much the same calculus, and if he had succeeded at anything it was in shielding the boy from this.

"We're doing well today, no?" the blind man said. He didn't wait for an answer, just smiled dumbly, then hummed a tune, snapped his fingers.

Then the light had changed, and the boy gathered himself and led the blind man again through the idling rows of traffic. The air was sweet with exhaust. A man, driving alone, dropped money into the tin. Maico stopped short. He turned to the blind man, faced him.

"What are you doing?" the blind man asked.

It wasn't a question Maico could have answered, even if he'd tried. There was no question of trying. Maico reached into his pockets, pulled out the money they had earned that morning, the money they'd been given, and dropped the first handful into the blind man's tin, where it rattled wonderfully, heavily, falling with such abrupt weight that the blind man nearly let go. What's wrong with you, boy, but Maico was not listening anymore, could hear nothing but the sound of the revving motors, and he watched in the glare for the light about to change; another half handful of coins, little ten cent pieces, the bigger silver ones that really meant something, all of it Maico dropped into the tin and he read confusion on the blind man's face and the money was all gone now, he had none of it, and he began to step back and away from the blind man.

"Where are you going? Where are you?" the blind man said, not pleading, but not unconcerned.

And Maico steeled himself, and with a swift slap, he upended the blind man's tin, knocking it and the coins from the beggar's hands and into the street. Some rolled under the idling cars, others nestled into the cracks in the pavement, and a few caught a glint of sun and shined and shined. But only for the boy. A moment later the light had changed, and the traffic had resumed its northward progress, but even if it had not, even if every car in the city had waited patiently for the blind man to drop to his knees and pick up each of the coins, there was something Maico saw that made it all worthwhile. It was what the boy would remember, what he would play over in his mind as he walked away, across the bridge and up the long, slight hill toward his home. The blind man, suddenly helpless – for a moment, he was not pretending.

X-24

unclassified

Laila Lalami

The Saint

Farid had saved her. Some people said it was impossible. They said the boy was only ten years old, that he could have barely saved himself, let alone his mother. They didn't believe Halima when she told them that he'd held out a stick and used it to pull her through the water all the way to the shore. They asked her how he got the stick and she said she didn't know. Crazy woman, they said, fingers tapping temples. You have to forgive her, they said, she's been through so much.

But other people believed her. Halima could have drowned with the others, they said. The captain had forced them out of the boat before they could get ashore. The water was cold, the current was strong, Halima didn't know how to swim. Yet Farid had pulled her to safety somehow. And even though the Spanish police were waiting for them right on the beach, at least they were alive. Besides, the boy had helped his sister, Mouna, and his younger brother, Amin, as well. They had *all* survived. Farid was a saint.

Even her husband, Maati, thought it was a miracle. When he'd found out she'd tried to cross the Straits of Gibraltar, he'd kicked the TV off its stand and smashed what remained of the dishes. He told everyone that if all Halima wanted was a divorce, then why didn't she just pay him, like he'd asked her? He'd have divorced her. And what's five thousand dirhams for a woman whose brothers work in France? They could afford it. But to take his children, to run away like this, to risk her life and theirs, well, those were clearly the actions of a crazy woman. Is it any wonder he beat her? But even a hemqa like Halima had done one thing right, he said. She'd given birth to his son, to Farid, and his little boy had saved her life. She was lucky.

AFTER HALIMA RETURNED to Casablanca, she didn't move back in with her mother, who had never agreed with her decision to leave, and who, Halima feared, would try to convince her to get back together with Maati. Instead, she borrowed money again, this time from one of her cousins, and took up a room with her three children in Sidi-Moumen, a slum outside the city. She couldn't find a janitorial job like the one she had before she left, so she joined the hordes of day workers at the market, spent her time squatting on the dirt road, waiting for a nod from someone who needed laundry washed or spring cleaning done. The vendors arrived first, their carts piled high with oranges or tomatoes or sweet peas. Then the buyers drifted through, haggled over prices, bought their food. After lunchtime the marketplace emptied slowly and by the time the afternoon prayer was called she'd get up and go home. Sometimes, when she couldn't get a job, when the sun beat down on her head until she thought it would whistle like a kettle, she grew angry with Farid. Why had he saved her? Why had he saved any of them? There wasn't any point in living when all you could do was survive.

Then one day, she managed to get one of the vendors, who'd cleared most of his cart by lunchtime, to give her his leftover ears of corn. She planned to barbecue them for dinner. She was fanning the fire with the rabuz when someone knocked at the door. Maati was standing on her doorstep, his body filling the narrow frame. His shirt was open to his chest, displaying hair that had started to go white. His eyes were bloodshot. Halima turned on her heel, scanned the room, trying to figure out where she could hide in such a small place. But Maati grabbed her wrist and, without moving, flipped her back toward him. She bit her lip, steeled herself for the blow. But Maati didn't hit her. He stuffed a piece of paper in her hand. "If this is all you wanted," he said, "now you have it." And, as if to punctuate his declaration, he spit on her. The phlegm landed on her shirt, but all Halima could see was the divorce paper, with the elegant penmanship and unmistakable signature of the 'aduls at the bottom. He turned around and left.

Halima stood, stunned. The fear that had knotted her stomach at the sight of her now ex-husband subsided, and in its stead she felt the rush of blood to her temples. This feeling of elation was entirely new to her. She had tried everything to get this piece of paper, and when she least expected it, it had been delivered right to her doorstep. What had changed Maati's mind? From her mother, Halima had heard that barely a month after she'd run away, Maati had tried to marry again, but the girl's parents had heard about what happened to Halima and turned him down. Maybe he wanted to erase her from his life and start again with someone else. But then she remembered the long train ride from Tangier back to Casablanca, when Farid had turned to her and said, "I wish Baba had divorced you the first time you asked." She'd chuckled at his comment, ruffled his hair with her hand, and turned to look at the scenery outside. Now she folded the sheet of paper carefully and slipped it inside her purse. Her hands still trembling, she put a kettle on the mijmar and made herself a pot of tea. Farid's wish had been granted. She had her divorce. She sat, her chin resting on her hand, thinking about what it meant. And she remembered the bleeding tree.

When Halima was five years old, her mother had come home from the market, excited about the news she had heard: There was a bleeding tree, a holy tree, in Rabat. She'd packed their lunch and they'd taken the train to the capital, riding in the fourth-class cabin, where farmers sat on wooden benches, chatting over their bags, their crates, and their chickens. It was Halima's first trip to the city, and she was disappointed by the quiet streets, the groomed lawns in front of government buildings. The bleeding tree stood in an otherwise sparsely planted lot across from the flower market, a few steps away from the police station. A dozen people were there already, some sitting, some standing. From them, Halima and her mother heard the story of the tree. A developer had intended to tear it down in order to make room for a high-rise, but when the workers tried to fell it, it started bleeding. The pilgrims showed up soon after, some collecting the blood-red liquid for use in concoctions, others using the site as a prayer area. Work had to be halted. Today, someone said, the city had dispatched a scientist to tell people that there was no miracle.

Halima and her mother maneuvered their way to the front line of the crowd, where they could get a better view of the scientist. He was a young man, little more than a teenager, his hair all fluffed up in an Afro like those American singers on TV. He wore a striped button-down shirt and bell-bottom pants. A pencil was tucked behind his ear. He stood, quietly eating sunflower seeds, until everyone settled down. Then he walked up to the tree, flicked open a Swiss Army knife, and made an incision in the trunk. He discarded the piece of wood and, pointing to the blood-red sap, he said that this was a normal substance made by this particular kind of eucalyptus. He called the tree a fancier name, something that sounded like French or Spanish. The tree had been making sap for a hundred years, maybe more. It was perfectly natural. There was no miracle. There was nothing to see. Go home, he said. People shifted on their legs, looked around at each other, but remained standing. The scientist shrugged and left. Foolish man, people said. What does he know about miracles? He sullied this holy ground. They pointed to the soft, humid earth, where sunflower seed shells remained, a testament of his passage through the shrine. Halima's mother ran her crooked fingers along the trunk and took some sap, collecting it in a recycled pill bottle.

After the trip to Rabat, Halima's mother returned to Casablanca, full of hope that her arthritis, which had been flaring up lately, would subside; that her prayers would be answered. Halima's father, who always sat on the corner divan smoking unfiltered cigarettes, shook his head and said she was crazy. For a while, however, Halima's mother did get better. She'd started knitting again, and the sound of her needles working formed a soundtrack to every evening for a month. But soon news came from Rabat that the developer had cut the tree down and started work on the new building. When the arthritis flared up again, Halima's mother said it was because the tree had been torn down.

Halima took a sip of her tea. She shook her head. There had been no miracle for her mother, and maybe there was none for her. Still, even if she were to believe those people who said she'd dreamt up the stick and the rescue, she couldn't bring herself to brush off Maati's change of heart. Only a miracle could make that man give her back her freedom. Sometimes, Halima thought, it was better to surrender to things one didn't understand. Her son Farid had given her back her life. Twice. She had to accept that he was different.

That night, when she and the children went to bed on the mat, she lay on her side, staring at him for hours, reliving his young life in her mind. She wondered if there was some other miracle she'd missed because she wasn't paying attention. There was the time when she was walking with him, hand in hand, on their way to the Lakrie market. A motorist made a sharp turn just as she'd stepped off the sidewalk, and his Honda careened toward her. Farid had pulled her back just in time. She'd stood on the pavement, her legs wobbling under her, one hand resting on Farid's shoulders and one on her chest, as though that could quiet the beating of her heart.

She closed her eyes and turned to lie on her back. This boy of hers was a mardi, a blessed child.

KHADIJA, THE NEIGHBOR, was the first to ask. She came to the house one evening, dragging her son Adnan by the hand, forcing him to sit next to her on the mat. She was quiet while Halima made her a pot of tea, using whatever mint and sugar she had left. Farid sat with them, while his brother and sister played a string game, making shapes that resembled beds or boats, passing the string back and forth. Halima served the tea, and after the customary small talk, Khadija fiddled with the ends of her housedress, bit her lip, and asked for the favor. She said her Adnan was about to take his grade school exams, that he needed help, a bit of luck. "He already flunked last year," she said. "If he flunks again this year, they'll expel him. Can you imagine, ya Halima? What will I do with him if he doesn't go to high school?" She slapped her cheek for good measure.

"Why don't you keep him home and make him study?" Halima asked, irritated with Khadija for making such a demand. Everyone knew that Adnan had a habit of skipping school to play football on the street.

"But maybe your son can give him a blessing," Khadija insisted. Halima shook her head. Khadija was undeterred. "Didn't you say that he saved your life? Didn't you say that he saved your children's lives?"

Halima nodded, regretfully. Farid rested his head against her arm, as if to comfort his mother for her mistake. She held her palms open before her. "He is only a little boy," she said. "Besides, if he could accomplish miracles, would we be living this way?"

"Let Farid bless my son," Khadija said. "Let him bring us some luck."

"If Adnan studied, he wouldn't need any luck," Halima muttered. Khadija didn't answer. Instead, she gave Halima a wounded look. The silence grew heavy, imposing, yet Khadija didn't make any attempt to leave. At last, Halima nudged Farid. He put out his hand, touched Adnan's head, all the while looking away. His first blessing and already an unwilling saint.

Halima was washing the dishes when Farid came up to her. "Is it true?" he asked.

"What?"

"That I'm a saint?"

"Curse Satan, child," she said, shaking her head. "That woman is crazy." She picked up the tray and took it to the kitchen. "Don't forget to take the trash out."

"So why did you ask me to touch her son?"

"Because that was the only way I could get her to leave. Didn't you see?"

Farid nodded.

"You don't mind, do you?" Halima said, reaching out to smooth her son's hair. "It can't hurt, right?"

Farid shrugged. "No."

"At least, this way, she went home happy."

Farid took the trash and walked quietly out. From the kitchen, Halima heard Amin and Mouna teasing him about the blessing. "Touch my nose," Mouna said, laughing. "I think it's running. It needs a little baraka."

"How about my butt?" said Amin. "Maybe my farts will smell like perfume."

Farid slammed the door, but their laughter didn't stop.

EVEN WITH A saint at home, Halima still had to make a living. Her mother had told her about a janitorial job twice a week at a lawyer's office, but when she went to ask she was told that the position had already been taken. So she started selling beghrir at the market. Every year, when people tasted the beghrir she made for Eid, they would compliment her on how fluffy they turned out. Occasionally she'd make a batch of mille-feuilles to entice students go back home from school. She enjoyed working for herself and was good at sales. Things were working out after all, she thought. Sometimes, on her way home from the market, she'd find Adnan playing on the street and she'd drag him by the ear all the way to his house, telling him that he'd received a blessing and he shouldn't waste it on football. Before long, Adnan would run home as soon as Halima turned the corner of the street, her raffia bag balanced on her head.

One day in June, Halima and her children came home to find Khadija waiting for them, a qaleb of sugar tucked under her arm. She gratefully pressed the qaleb in Halima's hand. Adnan had somehow passed his exams. Halima murmured her congratulations and turned to put her key in the lock. Khadija didn't go away. She stood so close that Halima could feel the woman's warm breath against her neck. Halima unloaded the raffia bag and held it against her hip. "Adnan must have worked hard," she said. Khadija didn't seem to have heard. She kept staring at Farid, an awed look on her face. Halima pressed her son's shoulders and guided him and his brothers inside the house before turning back to Khadija. "Uqbal next year. Insha'llah he'll have the same success."

Halima closed the door and heaved a sigh. "Now she's going to want more," she said. "And she's going to tell others."

Farid was already peeling the blue paper off the cone of sugar. He broke off three pieces and gave one each to his brother and sister before putting one in his mouth. He grinned. "You said it didn't hurt."

A WEEK LATER, Halima was mixing the dough for beghrir when she heard a knock. Mouna opened the door. Halima's mother, Fatiha, shuffled in, leaning on her cane.

"What are you doing here?" Halima asked, getting up.

"Can't I see my own grandchildren?" Fatiha answered, an indignant look in her eyes. "You never bring them around anymore, so your poor mother has to take the bus all the way here to see them." She took off her jellaba and sat down on the mat.

Halima was afraid of what the unexpected visit might mean. Would her mother try to convince her once again to go back to Maati? Would she ask her to stop selling food at the market and get a proper job? Whatever it was, Halima knew the visit could not mean good tidings. "Go play outside," she told the children.

"Wait," Fatiha said. She rummaged for something in her purse, pulled out a handful of sweets. "I brought some candy for them." Amin and Mouna rushed to get their shares, noisily unwrapping the sweets, comparing colors and flavors.

"Have some, Farid," Fatiha said, stretching her crooked hand out to him.

The boy shook his head. "I don't feel like candy."

"Well, at least come closer, let me look at you."

"I'm just going to play outside." He grabbed the deflated football and took off, trailed by his siblings.

Fatiha clicked her tongue. "Bad manners," she said.

"Can you never say anything positive?" Halima asked. It was just like her mother, she thought, to find fault with three sweet children like Mouna, Farid, and Amin. Fatiha pursed her lips and stayed quiet for a while, watching as Halima poured some batter onto to the stone griddle.

"Have you been to the doctor?" Halima asked.

"What for?"

"For your arthritis."

Fatiha grumbled something about having already gone to enough doctors.

"You should go again. These days, they probably have better medication."

"I don't need medication. I'll be fine," Fatiha said, her voice trembling. "Besides, why should I worry about myself when my own daughter doesn't care enough about me to let me have a little blessing?"

Halima shook her head. Her mother's knack for melodrama was something she'd never get used to. She could never get used to people who wanted others to help them out of their problems instead of relying on themselves.

She picked up the first beghrir and set it on the tray, then ladled more dough.

"We all care about you, Mmi," Halima said. "Here, have a taste."

Fatiha rolled up the beghrir and took a bite. "God, this is delicious."

"I'll take you to the doctor myself."

"I don't have the money to go to the doctor's."

"Don't worry. I'll pay," said Halima. She reached out and touched her mother's hand, as if to comfort her. Then she turned to watch the beghrir break into bubbles as it cooked. She did not notice the fading afternoon light that lengthened the shadows behind her, framing her body like the arches of a shrine.

X-24

Biographies

NIKI AGUIRRE was born in the US and has lived in Chicago, Ecuador, Cadiz and London. She studied English Literature at The University of Illinois and graduated with an MA in Creative Writing from Birkbeck. She is currently working on a collection of short stories to be published in 2007, tentatively titled *29 Ways to Drown*. Her first novel, *Transcending the Virtual*, is due to be completed later this year.

DANIEL ALARCÓN'S fiction and nonfiction have been published in *The New Yorker, Harper's, Virginia Quarterly Review, Salon, Eyeshot* and elsewhere. He is Associate Editor of *Etiqueta Negra*, an award-winning monthly magazine based in his native Lima, Peru. A recipient of a Whiting Award for 2004, Daniel's story collection, *War by Candlelight*, was a finalist for the 2006 PEN/Hemingway Foundation Award and his first novel *Lost City Radio* was published in February 2007. He lives in Oakland, California, where he is the Distinguished Visiting Writer at Mills College.

NAOMI ALDERMAN grew up in the Orthodox Jewish community of Hendon, in north-west London. She has a BA from Oxford University and spent several years working for an international law firm, including two years in Manhattan. In 2003, she took the MA in Creative Writing at the University of East Anglia. Her first novel, *Disobedience*, was published in 2006; it was read on Book at Bedtime and won the Orange Award for New Writers.

MOHAMMED NASEEHU ALI, a native of Ghana, is a writer and musician. A graduate of the Interlochen Arts Academy and Bennington College, Ali has published fiction and essays in *The New Yorker*, the *New York Times, Mississippi Review, Bomb, Gathering of the Tribes,* and *Essence*. He lives in Brooklyn, New York.

SEFI ATTA is a former chartered accountant and CPA, born in Lagos, Nigeria. Her short stories have appeared in journals like *Los Angeles Review* and *Mississipi Review* and her radio plays have been broadcast by the BBC. Her debut novel, *Everything Good Will Come*, was published in 2004. Sefi is a graduate of the creative writing program at Antioch University, Los Angeles and teaches at Meridian Community College and Mississippi State University.

TASH AW grew up in Malaysia and moved to Britain when he was 18. His first novel, *The Harmony Silk Factory*, won the 2005 Whitbread Award and Commonwealth Writers Prize for Best First Novel and is published in 20 languages. He lives and works in London.

JULIA BELL is a novelist and Lecturer on the MA Writing Programme at Birkbeck. She is the author of two novels: *Massive* and *Dirty Work*, both published by Young Picador in the UK and Simon & Schuster in the US, and the co-editor of *The Creative Writing Coursebook* (Macmillan 2001)

GAYLENE GOULD has been writing fiction and dreaming about writing fiction since young. An arts programmer and cultural critic, she has had numerous non-fiction pieces published in magazines and journals and is a regular critic on Radio 4's *Front Row*. *The Sacrifice* is her first published fiction piece.

PETER HOBBS was born in 1973, and grew up in Cornwall and Yorkshire. He studied at New College, Oxford. His first novel, *The Short Day Dying*, won a Betty Trask award in 2005 and was shortlisted for the Whitbread First Novel Award and the John Llewellyn Rhys Prize. It was followed in 2006 by a collection of short stories, *I Could Ride All Day in My Cool Blue Train*.

JENNIFER KABAT lives between London and rural upstate New York where she is just completing her first collection of stories, They Mimic Our Greater Selves. She writes about art, architecture and design and has contributed to the *Guardian, Wired, Metropolis, Wallpaper* and *New York Magazine*. She's also served as an editor at *The Face, Arena* and the American design magazine *ID*. In 2003 she received an MA in creative writing from the University of East Anglia.

LAILA LALAMI was born and raised in Morocco. She studied English in Rabat and London, and earned her Ph.D. in linguistics from the University of Southern California. Her work has appeared in *The Boston Globe, The Los Angeles Times, The Nation, The New York Times, The Washington Post* and elsewhere. She is the recipient of an Oregon Literary Arts grant and a Fulbright Fellowship. Her debut book of fiction, *Hope and Other Dangerous Pursuits*, was published in the fall of 2005 and has since been translated into five languages.

KEN NASH: In lieu of his dream of being a swash-buckling pirate, Ken became a itinerant cartoonist. His cartoons and illustrations have appeared in numerous publications throughout the world. He recently completed his first collection of short stories *The Brain Harvest: Autobiographical Narratives and Other Fictions.* Ken currently lives, writes and trims sails in Prague and along the Czech seacoast.

NII AYIKWEI PARKES is a Ghanaian writer and editor based in London. His poems and short stories have been published far and wide, and he was co-founder with Courttia Newland of the Tell Tales short story initiative. Nii is the fiction editor of *X magazine*.

CLAIRE SHARLAND is a graduate of the MA Creative Writing course at the UEA. Previously, she has studied mime in Paris, and worked as a life-model, cook, cleaner, aromatherapist and bookseller. She now lives in Norwich, teaching creative writing and working on a novel.

MECCA JAMILAH Sullivan's fiction has appeared in and/or is forthcoming in a number of publications, including *BLOOM*, *What I Know is Me*, and literary journals from Temple, Yale, and Columbia Universities. A recipient of various awards in fiction and playwriting, Mecca holds an M.A. in English and Creative Writing from Temple University, and is currently pursuing a Ph.D. in English Literature at the University of Pennsylvania.

T. TARA TURK is a playwright/fiction/screenwriter. She was a Van Lier Fellow at New York Theater Workshop, a screenwriting fellow in the Cosby Screenwriting Program and a selected participant in the Producer's Guild Diviersity Workshop. She has written several short films appearing in such film festivals as the Women In Film, the BHERC film festival and the Brooklyn Academy of Music film festival. She is working on her second novel.

CLARE WIGFALL was born in Greenwich during the summer of '76. She grew up in Berkeley, California and London, and now lives in Prague. Her debut collection of short stories *The Loudest Sound and Nothing* will be published by Faber and Faber in August 2007.